DEPARTMENT OF SPOOKS

A high-level diplomat, about to assume a vital posting at the United Nations, is being blackmailed. But if he goes to the police and prosecutes, his career will be finished. Even though the press can only report him as Mr. X, his well-known face will be clearly revealed to everyone in court. So Government special agent Mike Hammond is given his orders: 'Winkle this blackmailer out, and he's all yours. You're judge, jury — and executioner.'

ERNEST DUDLEY

DEPARTMENT OF SPOOKS

Complete and Unabridged

LINFORD
Leicester

First published in Great Britain

First Linford Edition
published 2011

British Library CIP Data

Dudley, Ernest.
  Department of spooks. - -
  (Linford mystery library)
  1. Extortion- -Fiction. 2. Suspense fiction.
  3. Large type books.
  I. Title
  823.9′14–dc22

  ISBN 978–1–4448–0852–0

Published by
F. A. Thorpe (Publishing)
Anstey, Leicestershire

Set by Words & Graphics Ltd.
Anstey, Leicestershire
Printed and bound in Great Britain by
T. J. International Ltd., Padstow, Cornwall

1

MASK OF BLACKMAIL

1

Colonel Selby's telephone call brought Mike Hammond to the office at the back of Whitehall at midday on the dot. Selby liked people to be punctual.

He was chewing inevitably at his pipe-stem, standing at the window overlooking Horse Guards Parade when Hammond entered.

Selby wasted no time at all getting down to cases

'You go this alone,' he told Hammond. 'Anything goes up the spout don't rely on the Department to lift a finger.'

Mike Hammond's hard-lipped-mouth twisted in a grin while the other put him in the picture.

No one in the Department, Selby explained, had suspected that Comte Charles Dulane harboured any sort of skeleton in his cupboard.

The Comte was a new Parisian diplomat, who had been in London for a term as special French representative and expert on the Mediterranean bloc. Now he was due shortly to take over a newly-created post for the Western Powers at United Nations.

Then Comte Charles Dulane's younger brother Raoul Dulane had dropped the bombshell. He had found out that the Comte was being bled white by someone unknown.

'A blackmailer who never had it so good,' Selby said.

If the Comte went to the police, he would have to prosecute, or no action could be taken. That would mean his going into the witness box. Even though he would be reported in the Press as Mr. X. a face as well-known as Comte Charles Dulane's couldn't be hidden from every-one in the court.

'It'd be curtains for his career,' Hammond commented.

'So,' Colonel Selby said, 'it's up to you. A job right up your dark alley.'

His yellow tombstone teeth grated on the pipe-stem. 'Winkle this blackmailer out, and he's all yours. You're judge and

4

jury and . . . executioner.'

The two men's eyes met across the tobacco-smoke wreathed desk, while the hum of traffic from Whitehall filtered into the office. This Comte Charles Dulane really was the white-headed boy, Hammond reflected, if the Department would go to these sort of lengths.

Underscoring the fact that even the Comte himself must never know that his secret had been revealed, Selby pulled out a dossier from the clutter of his untidy desk.

'Here's your only lead,' he said. The dossier was marled TOP SECRET with a name. Ruth Stratton.

Riffling through the pages, Mike Hammond noted the photos clipped from fashion-magazines. Ruth Stratton was a model. There was her description and background stuff; her address; a note that her favourite bar was *Ruby's*, behind Park Lane, popular with debs and models, the Chelsea crowd. This was the girl who had entangled Comte Charles Dulane in the web of blackmail. Ruth Stratton. All Hammond needed to know was, who was behind her? Who was the big wheel?

There were some other names in the file. Not much info on them: Johnny Austin, Dulane's personal secretary, who lived on the job at Dulane's house, The Turrets, Marlow. There was Theo Powell, who headed a Bond Street model agency, often employing Ruth Stratton. Nothing much on him — there'd been a record of bouncing cheques, but that was in the past. Divorced. Patronized a certain discreet house in Knightsbridge, where one or two of the girls worked for the Department of Spooks.

That same evening found Hammond at *Ruby's*. The girl was there; she was a silver-blonde. She was alone. She didn't talk to anyone, though one or two wolves tried to talk to her. She was an expert at the brush-off.

Next evening, Mike Hammond was at *Ruby's* again. So was the girl. There was no one with her this time.

Hammond made his way unobtrusively through the noisy mob and found what he wanted, a space against the bar next to the silver-blonde. Leaning forward, he asked Ruby herself — ageless, her mop of curls dyed fire-alarm scarlet, her large heavily-powdered breasts bulging over black lace — for a Scotch. After he had taken a drink, he patted his pocket, scowling to himself as if he had forgotten his cigarettes.

Then a voice said in his ear: 'If you're dying for a smoke, I could save your life.'

It was a low-toned, husky voice, with a liquid warmth that made you think of the stars low in a night sky over the Med. Her eyes were a smoky-blue, and her lashes were thick and black.

He smiled at her, a slow jagged twist of his thin lips, and took a cigarette from the thin gold cigarette case she offered him.

As he lit it, she let an eyebrow lift at his sun-tanned craggy face beneath jet-black unruly hair, the eyes like chips of grey ice, the bleak mouth and jutting chin.

He looked at her glass, which was practically empty, then he eyed her questioningly. 'That's nice of you,' she said. 'Gin's my sin.'

After he had ordered it for her, she said: 'Haven't I seen you somewhere?'

'You might,' he said. 'I've been there.'

He drew at his cigarette and caught her reflection in the mirror behind the bar, as she observed him speculatively. What he saw in the mirror was the face of danger. Yet her warm, curving mouth with the faintly mocking smile gave no hint there that this would be like handling dynamite.

She had been waiting for him to make the first move, he thought. But she could not know what he was there for.

His gaze drifted idly from the little amused expression she was wearing to the clock over the bar, which said 7.55.

'Going somewhere?' she asked.

He was sizing it up, deciding if he should take it any further tonight. He had made the contact, but if he tried to sew it all up too quickly, it might scare her off. Yet he couldn't dismiss the hunch that he shouldn't let this opportunity slip. Tomorrow might be too late.

She gave a look over her shoulder, and he followed her glance, but whoever it was she had seen must have gone. She was frowning as if someone had come in whom she hadn't expected to see.

8

He hesitated, then he said: 'There's a little place I know where we could eat.'

She shook her head. 'I already have a date.' She threw another glance over her shoulder. 'I thought I saw him come in. Must have been mistaken.'

The name of the man she was meeting, she said, was Theo Powell. No, he lied, he didn't know the name.

She said slowly, over the rim of her glass: 'I could push him out, I suppose. He's calling at my flat, but if you like to look in later, Theo will have gone.'

'I'd like that,' Mike Hammond replied.

She gave him the address. There would be coffee or a drink for him around 10 o'clock, she promised. She finished her drink, told Hammond she could find herself a taxi. He watched her figure curving alluringly, her legs slim above her stiletto heels, as she went out of the crowded bar.

Ruth Stratton got a taxi just outside *Ruby's*. But she didn't give the driver the name of the restaurant she had said she was going to, instead she gave the address of her flat. As the taxi moved off, a tall, thin man wearing dark glasses under the snap-brim of his black hat stepped out of the shadows of an empty shop next to *Ruby's* . . . He grabbed another taxi idling past and snapped a brief instruction to the driver.

Ruth Stratton in the corner of her taxi found her thoughts back at *Ruby's* and with the dark, craggy-faced man, a question mark forming in her mind. Back in London only a few days from the South of France and Rome, where Theo Powell had introduced her to fashion-houses offering her jobs over several weeks, she had experienced the feeling all the time that something was off-key. As if her every move was being observed by some secret watcher.

Even now she felt impelled to glance through the back window, as if scared she was being followed. She saw nothing, only another taxi way behind, and she pulled herself together. Outside the small block of flats in Palmer Street, off Oxford Street, she paid off the taxi and went through the glazed double doors. Her stiletto-heels tap-tapped across the black and white tiled floor of the entrance hall.

It was an old-fashioned building with no lift, and she went up to her first-floor flat. Shutting the front door behind her, she suddenly tensed. She felt sure she had closed the sitting room door when she went out. Now it stood half-open. Her heart began to race as she went in.

In the pool of light thrown by the table-lamp a shadowed figure on the settee faced her.

She gave a sharp gasp. The other stood up; he was wearing impeccable evening clothes. He was thickset, with heavy shoulders.

'I hope I didn't startle you,' he said softly, but his glance was cold as it hovered over her slender figure, her rounded breasts swelling up from her low-cut dress. He came towards her, a signet ring glinting on his left hand.

It was just 10 o'clock when Mike Hammond parked his souped-up convertible at the corner of Palmer Street. It was a narrow street, ill-lit, with the windows of the houses on the other side watching him with blank, dead eyes as he walked on past the entrance to the block of flats where Ruth Stratton lived. He retraced his steps, keeping his eyes skinned all about him.

The street appeared deserted. From the direction of Oxford Street came the rumble of the night traffic.

Hammond paused for a moment outside the entrance to the flats to give a look up and down. Then he went in. He went up the stairs, and his thumb was on the bell-push when he noticed that the front door of Ruth's flat gave a faint creak. He thought maybe she had left it open for him.

He went in. A whiff of scent, which he remembered was hers, reaching his nostrils. The sitting room door facing him was open, a glimmer of light from it seeping into the dark hall.

Mike Hammond stood in the doorway, his eyes travelling round the room until they were held by another door, which was half-open.

He moved quietly, his whole body relaxed, his brain razor-sharp, to the door of the bedroom. That was what it was, and her scent was stronger. He pushed the door wide and eyed the white and silver walls with their enormous mirrors and the mirrored ceiling. He had a sudden mental image of a wardrobe filled with sexy costumes, and a drawer or two filled with 'sex toys', and a certain type of cassettes, and other novelties. But his attention was focused on the figure sprawled on the white and silver bed.

He stood over it and saw the knife-hilt protruding from the man's thick neck where it had cut the external jugular vein. Blood was oozing over the white shirt and silk dinner jacket lapel. The eyes stared up at Mike Hammond sightlessly. The left hand on which the signet ring gleamed, hung loosely, touching the floor,

There was a time to stay and a time to go, Hammond told himself. This was no time to stay. He went quickly out of the bedroom, crossed to the door, and paused in the hall long enough to reassure himself he had touched nothing since he had entered the flat. None of his fingerprints would be left behind. He closed the front door quietly behind him and was hurrying, a lithe, muscular shadow, down the stairs and across into the street.

A glance up and down. No one to be seen, and he was walking swiftly towards Oxford Street.

Fifteen minutes later he had left his car in its garage and was back in his own flat in Jermyn Street, pouring himself a stiff slug of whisky.

He had to stay out of that business at Ruth Stratton's flat, that was for sure. His job was to sort out, and eliminate, Comte Charles Dulane's blackmailer without involving anyone else; the police, even the Department. 'You go this alone,' Colonel Selby had warned him.

Where was Ruth Stratton? And who was the man who lay dead in her bedroom? It seemed safe to assume, Hammond argued to himself, that he was known to her. She might have killed him; or, if she hadn't, she could know who had.

Had she invited him, Hammond reflected, along to her flat deliberately, knowing what he would find? He finished his Scotch and lit a cigarette and paced the room. What would be her motive for involving him in the murder?

Whatever it was, he had to make contact with her again, wherever she was. So an anonymous phone call to the police wouldn't help, the longer they took discovering the murder and getting on her track, the more time it gave him to find her first.

It occurred to him that she might have known nothing of what had happened. He recalled that there was this man, Theo Powell, who was calling at the flat. She could have gone out with him, and not got back by 10.

At that moment the front doorbell rang. Mike Hammond exhaled slowly; his grey eyes like chips of ice. He crossed to the battered-looking writing desk behind the leather armchair, unlocked a drawer and took out his snub-nosed Smith and Wesson Chiefs Special 2-inch barrel job. All the chambers were loaded with .38s.

He slopped the revolver into the soft leather holster specially built into his jacket under his left armpit.

He went out of the sitting room and opened the front door. The tall figure standing there wore dark glasses under his black snap-brim.

'I'd like a little chat,' the man said. 'It won't take up much of your time.'

Mike Hammond regarded the tall, thin figure for a moment. Then he shrugged and let him go into the sitting room. He gave a jagged smile at the dark glasses the other was wearing.

'Having trouble with your eyes?' he inquired.

'You're the one who's got trouble,' came the reply. The man was glancing around. 'You should be packing,' he said, 'ready to leave town before the police catch up with you.'

Mike Hammond's expression was frankly disbelieving.

'You think I'm kidding?' the other snarled.

There was a movement of his black-gloved hand from his pocket and he flipped a photograph onto the table between them. It was a blown-up glossy print. As Mike Hammond lowered his gaze a fraction to

16

see that it was a photograph of himself bending over that sprawled figure in Ruth Stratton's bedroom. He heard the man in dark glasses say:

'Comte Charles Dulane's brother, Raoul Dulane — *and the man who murdered him.*'

2

Staring at the photograph, Mike Hammond had a mental picture of Ruth Stratton's flat; the soft lighting, the scented atmosphere of sex. Behind one of her mirrored bedroom walls had been a secret cine-camera, noiselessly filming everything that happened there.

It all fitted into the blackmail racket that Ruth Stratton was involved in. Hammond wondered what sort of photographs there were of her and Comte Charles Dulane.

'I think I get your drift,' he said to the other. He could feel the eyes watching him from behind the dark glasses, glinting in triumph.

'You appear to be the sensible type.'

'Just as a matter of interest,' he asked the man in dark glasses facing him: 'Who did stab Raoul Dulane to death?'

'Haven't you guessed?' The black-gloved hand moved again and the glossy print was returned to his pocket. 'The girl, naturally.'

Hammond nodded as if it was the most natural thing in the world.

'It seems,' the other went on, 'he had some fanciful notion that she was putting the thumbscrew on his brother, the Comte.'

It was the answer Mike Hammond had been expecting. His thoughts coiled round Ruth Stratton, the smoky-blue eyes and warm mouth under the silver-blonde hair. Not the sort who would be expected to shove a knife into a man's neck up to the hilt.

That had looked more like the work of an expert, who knew his way around with a knife. Still, you never could tell. But, if she had killed the brother of the man she was blackmailing, what had been her reason?

The way he looked at it that would be the last thing she would want to do. A blackmailer was essentially a non-violent character. His whole object in life was to keep his victim alive — a living death, if you looked at it that way — but alive, and paying up.

He said to the tall man: 'So you happened to be passing, and you just dropped in to let me know that a girl I happened to meet for the first time tonight murdered Comte Charles Dulane's brother?'

'More than that. Whatever your business is with her, keep off the grass. Or else, this little lot — ' he patted his pocket ' — goes to Scotland Yard, and you can talk your way out of it from there.'

The tall, thin figure turned with a swift movement out of the sitting room into the hall. At the front door he turned, the dark glasses glinting menacingly under his black hat-brim. The door opened and he was gone.

Mike Hammond made no move to follow him. It was not the visitor who had just left who interested him. It was the big wheel who had sent the tall, thin man to warn him off, whom Hammond wanted to tangle with,

He had to admit that, whoever he was, he had played quite a smart card. That glossy photo of him looking as if he had been caught in the act of stabbing Raoul Dulane to death had only to be left at

Scotland Yard and he would have one hell of a lot of explaining to do.

And if he was going to complete the job he had been given he didn't want the C.I.D. breathing down his neck.

Hammond lit a cigarette and dragged at it. Ruth Stratton was the link, He had to find her, and fast. He realised that she would be taken care of by the setup in which she was involved. Wouldn't she have to stay under cover? But Scotland Yard would be checking up on the ownership of the Palmer Street flat. And then a sudden thought rocked him on his heels.

Supposing Raoul Dulane's corpse was removed from the flat? There was no need why it should be left there; it could easily be spirited away and dumped where it might not be discovered for days or weeks. It might never be found at all.

Raaoul Dulane, brother of the eminent politician Comte Charles Dulane, had disappeared; that's all the newspapers might say. And then, another thought hit Mike Hammond. Supposing nothing was reported about the dead man, nothing at all? The Department could take over and keep the whole thing quiet, until it suited them to release the news of young Dulane's death, somewhere abroad. Or he'd been drowned, washed out to sea while bathing in the Caribbean, anywhere that fitted.

Mike Hammond needed no reminder of the strings the Department could pull. He remembered Colonel Selby's instructions: *'You'll be judge and jury, and . . . executioner.'* Hammond had known then that the Department would go to any lengths to protect Comte Charles Dulane. Any lengths included keeping his brother's murder a secret, if it meant involving him to the risk of scandal.

Whichever way Hammond looked at it, he knew there was only one move he could make.

Twenty minutes later found him parking his convertible a little way from Palmer Street. He reached the small block of flats where Ruth Stratton lived. He walked quickly past the entrance, as he had done on his previous visit. He came to a side turning and went down it.

It was a cul-de-sac, pitch-dark. At the bottom a narrow passageway ran off at right-angles. It must run at the back of the block of flats.

This was how Mike Hammond aimed to make his next call at Ruth Stratton's flat — by the back door. Like a wraith he went along the passageway until it opened on to a small yard. Above it loomed the flats.

There was a sudden clatter of a dustbin-lid, and, as Hammond ducked into the shadows, a grey shape streaked past him. He had disturbed a scavenging cat. Or was it someone else, prowling in the darkness, who did the disturbing,

Mike Hammond hung back for a few moments. Then; as he was about to move forward, he sensed something ahead of him. It wasn't a cat this time,

A tall figure loomed up at him, moving fast. Hammond glimpsed the upraised arm aiming a glinting blade at his throat. Instead of attempting to turn aside, he moved in. His own right hand sped up, the hard edge of his palm smashing against his assailant's neck.

The tall shape seemed to hover over him as if suspended by invisible wires. Then it crumpled and fell flat on the face. Hammond bent, cutting a small radius of light from his pencil-torch, and saw the man's face.

The black hat was knocked aside, but the dark glasses still covered the eyes. Hammond whipped them off. He wanted to know what he looked like, this stranger he had met twice in the space of an hour.

The face, a thin trickle of blood at the corner of the mouth, meant nothing to Hammond, and he shoved the inert figure against the dustbins. The man wouldn't regain consciousness for an hour. Those judo blows really worked.

Mike Hammond was moving up the fire escape. At the top of the first flight was the door he wanted. It was locked, but next to it was a window. The pencil-torch showed the catch. Hammond's elbow swung. There was a crunch and tinkle of breaking glass, and Hammond was leaning through the opened window, unlocking the door.

He was in the kitchen, the thin wedge

of his torch-beam showing him an open door opposite. Swift, noiseless strides brought him into the tiny hall he knew from his previous visit. Once more that whiff of scent, which was Ruth Stratton's reached him. And the glimmer of light from the sitting room. He went in fast across the thick, wall-to-wall carpet. The bedroom door gaped, the light off. His fingers found the switch, and the white and silver walls and the mirrors leapt at him.

But this time there was no body of Raoul Dulane sprawled on the white and silver bed, a knife in his neck up to the hilt.

The body might never have been there. Hammond could have dreamed it. No sign of blood; the bedspread smooth, and creaseless.

Mike Hammond left the room and glanced back at the mirrored walls, wondering if the cine-camera was still turning, silently filming him from its secret place.

He was not particularly surprised to find the body had vanished. It explained the man in dark glasses, lying now against the dustbins. He would have taken care of the removal job and generally tidied up.

There was a movement at the sitting room door, and Ruth Stratton stood there.

She halted at the sight of him. Then she recovered her poise enough to smile: 'I wasn't expecting you.'

'To be dead honest,' he told her, 'I wasn't expecting you.'

'This happens to be my flat,' she said. She appeared frankly puzzled by his presence

'I'm sorry if I wasn't in when you called at 10. Did you?'

He nodded. She had moved in close to him, her scent subtly alluring.

'If you'd only hung around a little. I had to go out — er — unexpectedly. But I was back.'

'You left your front door open.'

Her smoky-blue eyes widened, and a frown drew her eyebrows together. She turned away from him with a shrug, then took a cigarette from the large silver box and lit it while he stood and watched.

She swung back on him. 'What's your racket?'

Her voice was low-toned and husky. He took a cigarette case from his pocket, and said, through a cloud of smoke: 'Right this very moment I'm interested in the murder of Raoul Dulane brother of Comte Charles Dulane, of whom you may have heard.'

It was as if he had struck her across the mouth. Her face went deathly white. For a moment he thought she was going to pass out.

Mike Hammond's eyes narrowed. This was no play-acting. Whatever else she knew, Ruth Stratton was ignorant of the body that had been lying in her mirrored bedroom. His fingers dug into her round shoulders, bruising the white flesh, as he began probing her with harshly incisive questions.

Her answers confirmed his impression that she was in the dark. She knew nothing of the murder of Raoul Dulane.

Her story was that when she had got back to the flat he had been awaiting her to her surprise, instead of Theo Powell.

She had met Raoul Dulane through the Comte, Ruth Stratton said. Yes, she admitted the Comte had been her lover. She knew he was married to a beautiful wife. But it had been one of those things.

Raoul Dulane had started accusing her of blackmailing his brother, she went on. She had denied any knowledge of this. In the middle of it all, Theo Powell had telephoned that he was waiting for her at a restaurant. His plans had been changed, but he wanted to see her.

She had told Raoul Dulane to wait while she hurried to the restaurant to see Powell. She would be right back.

But there had been no Theo Powell there. She had waited, but he failed to show, so she had returned to the flat. No Raoul Dulane, she told Mike Hammond.

By now the time was after 10 o'clock. She had decided Hammond had come and gone, and went off to Ruby's hoping to catch him there. The rest he knew.

'This Theo Powell?' Mike Hammond asked her, and he thought it unnecessary to mention that her description fitted exactly his visitor in the dark glasses and the man he had left out cold, at the back of the flats.

She was fixing him a drink and one for herself, while she told him how she had met Theo Powell with Johnny Austin, Comte Charles Dulane's secretary, and how he had helped her over her modeling.

She filled in the picture for him about Comte Charles Dulane, his beautiful English wife, Faith, and their riverside house down at Marlow. All she said confirmed his impression that she was merely the dupe of the brain behind the blackmailing of Dulane.

She was doing all the talking, and Mike Hammond let her do so, when he thought he caught a sound from the kitchen. He went out quickly. Had Theo Powell come round from that judo-blow more quickly than victims usually did? But there was no one. He stared down from the fire escape into the blackness of the yard. No one.

When he got back to the sitting room Ruth Stratton wasn't there, He tensed, and his gaze fastened on the door to the dark hall.

He swung on his heel as she came out of the bedroom, wearing a cloudy negligee. Her smoky-blue eyes and warm mouth were inviting over her drink.

The slow, jagged twist to his thin-lipped smile wasn't because he was remembering the silent cine-camera behind one of her mirrored bedroom walls, it was because he was thinking that with Raoul Dulane's corpse vanishing he was left in the clear over Scotland Yard seeing that photo of him and the body.

That took care of one headache, anyway.

It needed all his strength of purpose not to take Ruth Stratton at her word, unspoken, but written across her face like a big invitation to a marvellous party.

Shortly afterwards he was back at his Jermyn Street apartment. He had advised her to quit her flat and go into hiding somewhere until the danger that he warned her she might be in was over.

She hadn't taken him seriously at first, but he insisted. 'All right,' she said. 'I'll phone you tomorrow and tell you where I've gone.'

An uneasy feeling was assailing him. He glanced at his wristwatch, which said 12.45, and was deciding to phone her and warn her again, when his telephone jangled into life. It would be her, he thought, telling him she was taking his advice and giving her new address.

The cautious voice in his ear when he picked up the receiver was a man's. 'That Mr. Hammond? Mr. Mike Hammond?'

Hammond omitted to give the required information, instead he asked: 'Miss Stratton there?'

'She is; you want her to speak with you?'

'Just say a friend called.'

'Won't do much good, Mr. Hammond.' The voice was quietly insinuating. 'She wouldn't hear me. She's dead.'

Mike Hammond hung up,

3

In the instant that Mike Hammond turned away from the telephone a sound reached him from the street below. Switching off the light, he crossed to the window for a quick glance.

A black car that bore all the marks of a police vehicle had drawn up, and already two men in raincoats, hats tipped over their faces, were moving fast towards the street door leading up to his flat.

They could be police, just as the voice on the phone might have been that of a policeman, but they could be other people. Whoever they were, he was obviously the object of their visit.

Mike Hammond was in the hall, switching off the light and opening the front door. The rapid scuff of footsteps hurrying upstairs reached him, and he fisted his Smith and Wesson Chief's Special out of its soft leather holster under the left armpit of his jacket, and waited in the darkness behind the door, so that it would swing back on him.

The footsteps came with a muffled rush, and halted outside. 'It's open,' a voice said, the tone low.

'Maybe he's cut and run,' another voice answered in a mutter.

The door swung back cautiously on Hammond and a dark broad shape moved ahead of him.

Hammond let the visitor take a few paces along the darkened hall. His own eyes were accustomed to the darkness. Then, as the second figure came in and started to close the door, Mike Hammond clubbed the short barrel of the Smith and Wesson down on the base of the man's skull.

With an agonised grunt, the man collapsed. The other, his silhouette black and towering swung round and lurched at Mike Hammond.

He gave a yelp of pain as the muscular edge of Hammond's palm caught the side of his jaw, but he still came on. Hammond moved in close, bringing up his knee into the pit of the man's stomach. It was crude, brutal stuff, but Mike Hammond was expert in it.

Before the other's whistle of agony had started, his second judo-blow connected with the nape of the man's neck and there were two figures on the floor.

Snapping on the light, Hammond shoved both men into the bathroom opening off the hall, and locked the door. He switched on the sitting room light, to convey to anyone watching below that events in the flat were taking their anticipated course, and so that he could pack — fast.

Within a few minutes, locking and bolting his front door, Hammond was swiftly taking the tradesmen's stairs down from his kitchen, and heading for the all-night garage where he kept his convertible.

His car's dashboard-clock registered 1.23 as he raced through Shepherd's Bush, his destination Marlow.

He had two urgent reasons for getting out of town like a bat out of hell. One, Ruth Stratton's death would bring too many police or others buzzing round, like the pair of visitors he'd already had. Two, Comte Charles Dulane, his lovely English wife Faith, and his secretary, Johnny Austin, were at Marlow. Austin was a man who Mike Hammond thought it was about time he met.

As his giant headlights tunnelled the night, Mike Hammond's thoughts were full of Ruth Stratton, and that voice over the telephone, whose intonation had made it clear she had been murdered.

By whom? Theo Powell, whom he had left unconscious in the darkness at the back of the flats? He should have broken the other's neck while he had been about it, he told himself grimly.

After all, he had warned the girl; and, anyway, he had enough on his plate sorting out the blackmail tangle that Comte Charles Dulane was caught in. But his eyes like chips of grey ice were slitted vengefully as he drove on through the night.

It was still dark when he hit Marlow's outskirts, and he parked in a side road, preparatory to grabbing some sleep. He didn't want to attract attention to himself

35

arriving at an unearthly hour.

Mike Hammond breakfasted at a roadside café and drove into Marlow, where he got himself a room at a quiet pub, the *Kingfisher*.

His car radio had given him the news that the police were seeking a man believed to have been in the vicinity of a flat off Oxford Street where a fashion model had been found dead. He read about it in the Stop Press of the morning paper in the Riverview Bar where he found himself later that morning.

The Riverview Bar was where the local smart crowd got together for that pre-lunch snorter, or to work off that old hangover.

From his seat in the corner, Hammond took the crowd in — the pretty girls, the nattily-dressed, fast-joking young men. He had Ruth Stratton's description of Johnny Austin to go by. He was always at the Riverview Bar around lunchtime.

Mike Hammond spotted him. Blond wavy hair, horn-rimmed glasses, a thin, two-inch scar running down from his left eye.

Taking his drink as if looking for someone, Hammond made his way towards Austin and the couple of other men with him at the bar.

One of them was saying as Hammond came within earshot: 'That white sports-job of yours is new, isn't it Johnny?' And Austin smiled and nodded.

The other went on: 'Makes a change from that old heap you used to run around in. What happened, some rich old aunt leave you a fortune?'

But the other wasn't listening. His sleepily amused glance behind his horn-rims suddenly changed as it fixed Mike Hammond. For a flash Hammond had the impression that Johnny Austin thought they knew each other.

It was an odd sensation, but Hammond knew he'd never set eyes on him before, even as the horn-rims turned away for Austin to make some evasive remark to his companion.

In the crowded car park, Mike Hammond, climbing into his convertible, indicated a white, expensive-looking sports car to the car park attendant. 'Isn't that

Johnny Austin's new job?' he asked casually.

The man nodded. 'Smashing job, eh? Set him back a packet, I'll bet.'

Hammond drove off, mulling over the thought that even a private secretary to Comte Charles Dulane didn't find that sort of money growing on trees.

It could mean nothing; it could mean something. It could mean Johnny Austin had recently received a fat wad of money from some source.

Later that afternoon, Mike Hammond drove out of the town beside the river a couple of miles, made a right-hand turn down a narrow road overhung for half a mile by massive trees, until he found himself outside tall iron gates. They were locked.

Leaving his car, he went a hundred yards along under the high wall until he came to a door. It, too, was locked; but several seconds' tinkering with his skeleton keys did the trick. The door creaked open, and beyond lay The Turrets, Comte Charles Dulane's English home.

Hammond forced his way through a

tangle of shrubs and bushes until he reached a cleared path. All about him trees and shrubbery grew thick, weed-infested. He set off in the direction of the house, and had proceeded a short distance when the path widened.

A sixth sense halted him for a moment. He seemed to be able to sniff danger on the dank air. He went on, the trees and bushes still thick on either side.

Then the path suddenly twisted. Across an expanse of smooth lawn he saw the house, dark brick and turreted like a miniature castle.

The afternoon light had darkened, a black mass of cloud was spreading up from the horizon beyond the river, and the house took on a gaunt, brooding appearance.

A balustraded terrace ran along it, on to which tall French windows opened. Beyond the house a line of willow trees indicated the riverbank.

Mike Hammond decided to see what the other side of The Turrets looked like. It might be a little more inviting, he thought.

It would be best to stick to the edge of the tangled plantation through which he had come, for he didn't want to show himself yet.

Already, he was experiencing the feeling that he was the object of some unseen scrutiny. And then, as he moved forward, a figure came through the French windows and stood on the terrace, staring straight across.

It was a woman, slim and tall. A shaft of light pushing through the mass of cloud picked her out, so that Hammond might have been looking at her photograph.

It was Faith Dulane, the Comte's beautiful wife. For a moment, Hammond could have betted she had seen him, even though he had stepped back into the shadows of the trees behind him.

He had seen her face in the glossy magazines, and even from this distance she didn't disappoint in the flesh. She looked fabulous, with a hauntingly appealing quality about her.

If Faith Dulane had seen him, she gave no sign. She turned and went back into the dark-looking house.

For a moment, Hammond had the impression she was held prisoner in there. He began moving again, keeping close to the trees.

The sense that he was being watched grew, so that he jerked a look at the house to see if the tall, slim woman was observing him from within. She could have been, but he couldn't see her.

Then he halted, every nerve taut. He had caught the faint swish-swish of something moving behind him. The sound had stopped when he did. He stared into the trees and tangle of shrubbery, but there was nothing.

He went forward again, and at once that stealthy swish-swish reached him. He stopped; it stopped. He went on again, and whoever or whatever it was that was keeping pace with him, went on also.

Hammond felt a crawling sensation under his scalp. Only a few feet away in the weed-choked bushes and trees, his unseen adversary stalked him.

A glance at the house showed that the terrace continued round it, broken by two short flights of wide steps leading up from the lawn which ran on down to the river's edge. A sudden movement ahead of him brought Hammond's eyes round with a jerk, and a crouching shape and low growl halted him in his tracks.

A massive dog had appeared in his path, an outsize specimen.

It had been tagging him, this was what he had heard alongside. It seemed, Mike Hammond reflected grimly, that Comte Charles Dulane didn't exactly welcome visitors,

He took a step forward and the ominous growl changed gear into a blood-curdling snarl and the animal launched itself at Hammond.

Hammond knew what would happen to him if he didn't act swiftly and decisively. The Smith and Wesson was out of its holster in a reflex action, Mike's finger squeezing the trigger.

The .38 special cartridge was a man-stopper, especially from that short range, but as the short barrel roared and the butt kicked in his fist Mike Hammond experienced a heart-freezing moment as the dog still came at him.

42

He knew he must have hit it but the bullet must have smashed clean through its heart and the great red-eyed brute's own savage impetus still carried it forward, the vicious fanged jaws reaching for Hammond's throat.

And then, as the slashing shape arched in mid-spring, a tremendous report rattled Hammond's eardrums, and the beast seemed to disintegrate before his eyes in shattered bone and blood.

Mike Hammond spun round at the figure stepping out of the shadow of trees and shrubs, a smoking shotgun aimed menacingly at his stomach.

The man whose thick finger curled round the trigger, and whose eyes seemed to hold a maniacal gleam, was Comte Charles Dulane.

The whiplash thought struck Mike Hammond that it was the Comte who had been stalking him and had meant to kill him, but had blown the dog to bits by mistake. He heard the click of the repeating shotgun's lever action, and the butt came up to Comte Charles Dulane's shoulder.

4

'Don't move,' Comte Charles Dulane rapped in impeccable English. 'Or I'll blow you to Kingdom Come.'

He was a more mature version of his younger brother, Raoul Dulane, of medium height, with broad-browed distinguished features. He was wearing a chunky tweed suit.

Mike Hammond kept his hands raised. The eyes behind the shotgun-sights were narrowed grimly enough, though they seemed to have lost their maniacal glint. Perhaps the glint had been merely a trick of the light as the dark, heavy clouds moved across the late afternoon sky.

This was the top-notch Parisian diplomat, Comte Charles Dulane, who had been a fashion-model's secret lover, Hammond reflected, and was being blackmailed on account of that indiscretion.

He didn't look as if he was having the

thumbscrews put on him. He didn't look worried; though you weren't supposed to know what a high-up diplomat was really thinking. Right at this moment he looked as if he'd let fly with the shotgun at the drop of the hat.

'You wouldn't happen to know that this is private property?' His voice, which bore no trace of accent, was clipped and quietly controlled.

Mike Hammond eyed him. He hadn't expected to meet up with the blackmailer's victim this way, with himself at the receiving end of a gun.

'If I'd known it was so well guarded,' he said, 'I wouldn't be here.' He glanced at what was left of the huge dog that had attacked him.

'My wife's idea,' the other said, 'there have been too many burglaries round here lately.' He gave a slight shrug. 'Well, it was either him or you.'

'For a moment,' Hammond said softly. 'I thought it was me.'

There was a brief silence while the Comte surveyed him carefully.

The Frenchman's expression had changed.

Now it held a look of speculation, as if, Mike Hammond wondered, the man's preconceived ideas about him had changed? Perhaps he had taken him for a tramp at first, and had decided he didn't quite measure down to that.

Hammond waited while the Comte continued to stare at him silently. He would have given a lot to know what was ticking away behind that broad, intelligent-looking brow. Did he, Hammond wondered, suspect him of having some part of the blackmail racket?

'You live in Marlow?' the Comte asked.

Mike Hammond said he was spending a day or two in the vicinity and named the pub he was staying at.

The gun lowered; there was a nod from its owner. Hammond put his hands down.

'Thanks,' he murmured, 'for saving my life.'

He turned away and retraced his steps along the edge of the trees and shrubs, conscious that Comte Charles Dulane still stood, his gun pointing in his direction.

Suddenly there were quick footsteps

behind him. Hammond swung round. The Comte was coming for him, the shotgun aimed once more at his stomach. 'Not so fast,' he grated.

Hammond shrugged. 'I thought you didn't care for trespassers on your property?'

'I'm not satisfied you are an ordinary trespasser.'

'So what are you going to do about it?'

The gun wagged at him. 'Take you into the house, and get the police.'

This wasn't going to be too funny, Mike Hammond thought.

Assuming that Scotland Yard was anxious to talk to him about Ruth Stratton's murder, his description would have been flashed to every police H.Q. in the country, airports, seaports — the full drill.

Marlow police, like the rest, would be on the lookout for him. Once they had him inside, he would find it tricky talking his way out again. Anyway, it would take time, and that was something he hadn't a lot of.

He needed to winkle out and deal with

the big brain swiftly, before whoever it was dealt with him.

'We'd better be moving,' Comte Charles Dulane was saying. 'And any funny business, and you'll get it where it'll hurt most.'

'You'd hardly be able to miss from where you're standing,' Hammond told him affably.

The gun indicated that he should raise his hands and move ahead. The other kept strategically behind him, Hammond sensing the shotgun aimed at the small of his back.

They crossed the lawn and went up the short flight of wide steps on to the terrace. As they paused there for a moment, Comte Charles Dulane called out, 'Faith.'

She appeared at the French windows, the tall, slim woman Mike Hammond had seen earlier. She gave a gasp, her eyes widening, but her husband's tone was calmly reassuring.

'It's all right. I caught him hanging about. Don't like the look of him. I'm going to call the police.'

Mike Hammond's thin lips twisted in a jagged smile at her. She stared at him, and it was just about the loveliest face he had ever seen.

Heart-shaped, her mouth softly pink with a crimson edge where her lips merged into her pale peach skin. The top corners of her eyelids were drawn back from deep violet eyes by a black line tapering up into the soft skin beneath her eyebrows.

She was fabulously slim, her legs long and slender in sheerest stockings.

'Where's Johnny?' her husband was asking. 'Not back yet?'

She shook her dark head. The husband glanced uncertainly from her to Hammond, who guessed that there was no one else in the house. Johnny Austin, the blond wavy-haired secretary in the horn-rimmed glasses, whom Comte Charles Dulane had referred to, hadn't returned from his lunch-date with his pals. And it looked as if this was the servants' afternoon off.

Hammond was tired of keeping his hands raised, but they jerked up again at the snarled: 'Keep them up, blast you!'

Mike Hammond smiled to himself, as he detected in the blustering tone a certain amount of doubt.

The Comte could be wishing he hadn't taken on the job of handing Hammond over to the police, after all. Perhaps it was beginning to occur to him that the publicity that might arise wasn't to be relished.

Mike Hammond speculated quickly on how he could turn the other's indecision to his advantage. The slightest false move and he knew he would be shot down where he stood.

His gaze flickered to Faith Dulane, but she had turned her look on her husband.

If only Hammond could reach his own Smith and Wesson nestling in the holster under his left armpit. He calculated he could turn the tables; even if it meant putting a bullet through the fleshy part of his arm.

He was about to risk it, when Comte Charles Dulane said to his wife: 'Take this, my dear.'

His tone was obstinate as he handed her the shotgun while still aiming it at

Hammond. She took it hesitantly, but Hammond noticed that she handled it as if she was used to sporting guns all right.

'While I call the police station,' her husband went, on. And he said to Hammond: 'My wife's a good shot, too, so don't think it'll be easier with her.'

'Thanks for the warning.' Mike Hammond grinned at him laconically.

He kept his hands raised. He fully believed what her husband had said, as the slimly lovely woman stood there, pointing the gun at him. She looked perfectly relaxed.

Her small white hands holding the gun were all set to let him have it if he asked for it.

The Comte gave his wife a quick, comforting smile and then went in through the French windows. A few moments later, Hammond heard the sound of the telephone receiver lifted, and then that clipped voice speaking crisply.

He was suddenly asking himself if Dulane had some ulterior motive for handing him over to the police. He recalled that switch in his attitude after he had started to take his leave; how the other had come after him.

Had he guessed what Mike Hammond was there for, and had he some private reason for throwing a spanner in the works?

Hammond was convincing himself that there was more to this blackmail business, so far as the supposed victim was concerned, and he was trying to work out what sort of job he had taken on, when Faith Dulane moved towards him.

The gun lowered, she spoke in a hurried whisper.

'Quickly — now's your chance.'

He stared at her, ice-grey eyes narrowed incredulously. 'What the — ?'

'I know who you are,' she murmured, with a quick glance through the French windows. 'I know you're trying to help my husband.' She was gabbling urgently.

'You must forgive him, he — he's not himself — but you must get away, *now*. You will have to hit me, to make it look convincing — '

He frowned at her, but she was close to him, her lovely face a mask of entreaty.

'I will tell you everything, later,' she whispered, 'At 6.00, at the boathouse, the old boathouse, further along the riverbank. Only go quickly — hit me, now!'

She meant it. The words hissed between her white teeth as she offered him her small, rounded chin.

He stared at her for an instant. There came a movement from the shadows beyond the windows, and he stepped in and smacked Faith Dulane across the jaw, catching the gun as she swayed and sank to the floor.

Her eyes were closed He wondered if she really was out cold, or was shamming realistically. Then, taking the gun with him, he ran for it.

There was a desperate shout behind him as he was halfway across the lawn. He didn't look back as he streaked into the tangle of trees and bushes.

A few minutes later, Mike Hammond had emerged from the door in the high wall and was walking swiftly along the road. He had disposed of the shotgun in some shrubbery.

Now, as he headed back to his car, he

kept his ears alert for the sound of any car. A car might bring the Marlow police. But the road remained empty, and he reached his convertible, parked where he had left it by the tall iron gates.

He got in, reversed quickly and accelerated up the narrow road, so dark under the overhanging trees and the gloomy sky, that he switched on his headlights. Still no sign of any police hurrying to The Turrets Hammond's mind went back to Faith Dulane. Maybe she had persuaded her husband to withdraw the story he had given the police.

What had prompted her to take the action she had? Had she really believed him to be a harmless individual whom Comte Charles Dulane had wrongly suspected? But she had told him that she knew who he was and what he was there for. To help her husband.

That suggested she was aware of the Comte's deadly entanglement. She might even guess that he was a victim of blackmail.

If she had learned the Comte's secret,

then she might have stumbled upon the identity of the brain behind the blackmail plot. She could tell him, she could help him winkle out that figure from the shadows who had instigated the murder of Raoul Dulane and Ruth Stratton.

Was this why she had urged him to meet her later?

Hammond's mind switched to the impression Comte Charles Dulane had given him — that he was alerted to the object of Hammond's visit to The Turrets.

It was as if he was playing some crafty game on his own, using his own rules. What mattered was whose side he was on?

Mike Hammond scowled to himself, trying to sort out the mix-up of conjecture and speculation, which needled him. He was halfway along the road when he felt a movement from the back seat. The hood was up; something was leaning over his shoulder out of the gloom and prodding his jaw with icy fingers.

From the corner of his eye he saw it was just that, a hand, limp and chill had appeared from behind him.

Mike Hammond braked to a stop, and slowly turned his head. The hand fell back as he leaned over and stared at the crumpled shape that had been shoved into the back seat.

He knew the face whose sightless eyes looked up at him.

5

It was Theo Powell who stared up unseeingly at Mike Hammond from the back of the convertible. This time wasn't wearing any dark glasses. A knife was stuck up to the hilt just below the nape of his neck.

It was not the sort of thing any man would want to have found in his car, least of all Mike Hammond, with Scotland Yard, and probably the local police, out looking for him:

Hammond switched off his headlights, and the narrow road lay dark in the tunnel of overhanging trees. He got out of the car and glanced back. He recalled passing an opening in the tall hedge with what might be a ditch beyond.

A few moments later he had reversed and stopped the convertible at the spot and was hauling the body out, lugging it through the hedge and into the ditch. There was nothing of any importance in the dead man's pockets, which Hammond went through with the aid of his pencil-torch. Some money, and the fact that the gold wristwatch was still there indicated that robbery had not been the murder motive.

Raoul Dulane, Comte Charles Dulane's brother had been similarly stabbed to death. And probably Ruth Stratton, though it had been kept quiet in her case. But that had happened in London.

Was the murderer now at Marlow? Had he followed Theo Powell down there? Why had it been necessary to eliminate him?

The answer could only be that he knew too much for somebody else's health. Who? That was the jackpot question.

Mike Hammond got back into the car. The dashboard-clock was coming up to 5:30. Hammond's meeting with Faith Dulane was in half-an-hour. This Theo Powell business had delayed him, he would not be able to get back in his pub, the *Kingfisher*, and check out, as he had planned.

Then Hammond recalled that he had

mentioned to Comte Charles Dulane where he was staying, though omitting to explain that he was using an assumed name. But the local police could be keeping the pub under observation.

Hammond came to the main road, cutting out his headlights. It was less dark, though the early evening sky was still overcast.

He kept his sidelights on. Still no sign of any police car racing to The Turrets. He turned left and proceeded along the main road a quarter-of-a-mile until he reached a narrow bridge. He pulled the car into the side of the road, got out and took a look round.

The bridge spanned a backwater running back from the river. Below a towpath ribboned along the bank in the direction of, as he worked it out, the old boathouse where Hammond was to meet Faith Dulane. He noticed a telephone-box beside the bridge, and opened the door. The light wasn't working, but Mike got through to the *Kingfisher*.

He gave his assumed name. 'I phoned to know if anyone had been asking for me,' he said to the landlord.

'No, sir: no one's been asking for you.'

The reply was unhesitating. The man didn't sound guarded or dissimulating. Hammond replied that he wouldn't be back till late and hung up. He decided to move out that night, anyway. It might prove healthier.

Turning over in his mind what game Comte Charles Dulane was really up to, and where his lovely wife came into it. Hammond made his way down the bank to the towpath.

The water, dark and oily-looking in the leaden light swirled past. As he went along the path, Mike Hammond's speculations turned to Ruth Stratton. his first link with the blackmailing setup, who had died because she had talked too much. To him.

If Theo Powell had silenced Raoul Dulane because he too, knew too much, it fitted that he had dealt with Ruth Stratton. Which brought Hammond back to this question: Who disposed of Theo Powell? Someone who had deliberately copied his method of using a knife.

A mist was beginning to uncurl across the dark water. The sky was heavy with foreboding cloud. Now, a couple of hundred yards ahead, Mike Hammond made out a long, low building running down to the water's edge. This would be the old boathouse Faith Dulane had told him about.

He paused for a moment, wondering if what he had just glimpsed was some trick of the eye. A brief flicker of light it had seemed, as if someone had used a cigarette lighter.

Was she there already, waiting for him?

The light did not appear again. Hammond moved on, but more cautiously, his footsteps noiseless on the grassy path, his eyes searching the enveloping gloom.

The boathouse was dark-timbered, obviously derelict as he could see when he drew nearer the sagging roof.

He could hear no one, no movement in the gloom, only the slap-slap against the sides of the boathouse which reached the water. Or was there a faint creaking noise inside? A loose board stepped on by someone. Faith Dulane? Or someone else? Faith's husband, for instance. He could have dug it out from his wife that she had a date with Mike Hammond.

Eyes narrowed in his craggy face, he turned aside, moving swiftly and silently to the bask of the structure and the dark rectangle which was the doorway.

The faint creaking sound reached his ears again. There was something in there, something waiting for him. Every sense, every nerve warned him of this. The Smith and Wesson in his fist was reassuring, but as he reached the doorway he would present a perfect target, silhouetted against the sky, for anyone within.

Hammond went in and. ducked low, but there was no gun-flash stabbing the darkness. No bullet smacked above his head.

Instead, there was a figure swinging from a beam. Creak-creak . . . creak-creak . . . It was a slim shape hanging there — that of Faith Dulane.

Hammond kicked aside a box as he reached her and, supporting her, relaxed the rope sufficiently to loosen the noose around her neck. In a moment he had it unlooped over her head, and stretched her out on the rotting floor.

Her heart was beating strongly. Resting her head against his knee, he gently massaged her throat. In a few moments she stirred convulsively. Her eyes opened and she gasped painfully up at him: 'What — what happened?'

'You've got nothing to worry about,' he said. 'Except a sore throat.'

'I was — I was waiting for you.' She struggled painfully to get the words out. 'I heard someone outside — I thought it was you. Then — then I must have been knocked on the head — '

Her voice trailed off in choking gasps. 'Don't try to talk if it hurts,' he told her.

She clutched at him, her dark hair subtly scented, brushing his face as he bent to support her with his arm. Her waist was incredibly slim beneath the curve of her breast.

'You — you've got to know.' she said, one small white hand at her throat. 'You are in danger yourself.'

He gave her a faint, jagged smile.

'That's all part of my job.' He paused, then: 'But who would want to kill you?'

He glanced behind him. A boat could have sneaked in while she was watching the door for him to show up. She wouldn't have heard anyone behind her, until too late.

'I — I — that is — you won't understand this,' she gasped. 'But — I'm almost sure it — it was my husband.'

Mike Hammond's eyes, like chips of grey ice, glinted in the darkness. This could be the answer to the blackmail plot, the murders. A smokescreen to cover up some fantastic ulterior motive of Comte Charles Dulane's.

A man in his position could have a dozen different reasons for pretending he was victim of a blackmail plot. It didn't even have to be a sane motive. Hammond recalled that maniacal light in the other's eyes earlier. But at that time he had decided it was merely a trick of the light.

'That's why I let you get away,' she was saying. 'I — I knew you were trying to — to help him, because he's in some danger.'

'Have you ever said anything about this to anyone else?'

She hesitated. Then she said slowly, still painfully: 'It was wrong of me, perhaps, but I spoke about it to his brother, Raoul — '

'When was this?'

'Two weeks ago, it would be.'

It fitted with what had happened. Raoul Dulane had taken her suggestion seriously. Perhaps he'd made a discreet inquiry or two on his own; then he'd gone to the office off Whitehall, and this was where Mike Hammond had come in.

By the way she was talking, Faith Dulane knew nothing of Raoul's death. This fitted into the jigsaw, also. The whole damned jigsaw fitted into place. Her husband could have murdered his brother, then Ruth Stratton. And that very afternoon, Theo Powell.

'What — what I'm afraid of,' the woman was saying, 'is that — that he's gone out of his mind.'

Her dark head lay against his shoulder, her slim waist curved under his hand. 'The strange way he's been behaving, as if he's — he's afraid of something. Or someone.'

Was this the answer? Was it some persecution-mania, Mike Hammond asked himself, that had impelled Comte Charles Dulane to kill, and kill again? Then where did Ruth Stratton's Palmer Street flat fit in, with its secret cine-camera?

Faith Dulane was murmuring that she should be returning to the house, when Hammond thought he caught a sound outside.

He left her while he stood at the door, listening. The sound, as if someone had moved, didn't come again. He could have been mistaken, and he came back and helped Faith Dulane to her feet. She swayed against him.

'If he's tried to kill you once.' he told her, 'he'll try again.'

She nodded. 'I must get away. Tonight. Back to London — I have friends who will keep me out of danger, until — until all this is settled.' Her violet eyes were full of appeal in her wan face.

'Perhaps — if you could see him? After I've gone, you see, he'll be alone. He's sent the servants away — and his secretary, Johnny Austin — ' she broke off helplessly.

'What about him?'

'It's only that he's been so loyal to my husband. He won't leave him — '

'You think he may be in danger?'

Hammond warned her grimly to look after herself. Warn Austin if she could, but get away from The Turrets as quickly as possible, without arousing her husband's suspicion.

He tried to persuade her not to go back, but let him drive her to London that evening. But she insisted she must show herself to her husband, try to test out if it was he who had attempted to murder her, and warn Johnny Austin.

Mike Hammond made no promise to her about his line of action. He had told her nothing of what he knew about the blackmail setup, Raoul Dulane's murder, Ruth Stratton, or Theo Powell.

His arm round her waist, he accompanied her through the shrouding mist to the lawn, across which the dark house loomed uninvitingly. He watched her move quickly over the lawn, like some tall, slim wraith, and hurry up the steps to the terrace.

She went into the house, without a glance back.

Twenty minutes later. Mike Hammond was driving into Marlow. He was telling himself that this looked like the end of the trail. Comte Charles Dulane filled his conjectures as the life-size culprit, insanely removing anyone he thought stood in his path.

There were loose ends to the unravelled tangle, Hammond was forced to admit, and they nagged at him as he parked the convertible a short distance from the *Kingfisher*. He walked quickly towards the pub, his eyes skinned for a sign of any police.

He seemed to be in the clear. He could slip up unnoticed to his room, pack, pay his bill and be away before it was realised he had come and gone. He went in and up to his bedroom unobserved. But as he turned the handle of his door some sixth sense rang a warning bell at the back of his skull that something was wrong.

The room was in darkness except for some light from the street lamps seeping past the drawn curtains.

He fingered the switch and as the room sprang into light he saw a figure in the chair facing him coolly.

The visitor was holding a gun in his hand.

6

Mike Hammond heeled his bedroom door shut behind him, his hands raised nonchalantly. Johnny Austin, the Comte's secretary, was the man behind the automatic. His horn-rimmed glasses glinted and a scar showed white two inches down from his left eye.

'To what do I owe this unexpected pleasure?' Hammond said.

The blond head shifted, the eyes behind the horn-rims smiled a little. 'Comte Charles Dulane, you could say. And one or two others.

'Living or dead?'

'Let's concentrate on the living.'

'The dead interest me,' Mike Hammond rasped 'They'll need to be accounted for.'

The other shrugged. 'Who interests you most at this moment? Who's most recently dead?'

'He went by the name of Theo Powell.'

Johnny Austin's face went blank, the

70

gun in his hand drooped.

Hammond dropped his hands and lit himself a cigarette. Austin raised his head and said across the room: 'When was this?'

Hammond eyed him through a cloud of cigarette-smoke. How much, he asked himself, did Austin know that he knew? The hunch that had been building up in his mind strengthened a trifle. The other said:

'You think I did it?'

Hammond glanced at the automatic. With a bitter smile Austin pushed the weapon into his pocket.

'I couldn't be sure how you'd take my being here, uninvited,' he said, as if by way of explanation.

'When I saw you in the Riverview Bar this morning, I decided you weren't there just having a quiet drink. Yours was a face I hadn't seen around before. I managed to get a look at your car, it was a London registration number . . . ' He hesitated and then went on: 'I've been developing a bit of a suspicious mind lately. I've been finding out things.'

'What things?' Mike Hammond asked softly, 'for instance?'

The other looked at him speculatively. 'I'm the Comte's confidential secretary,' he said. 'I've been with him the past several years in Paris and London.'

Hammond had suddenly turned his head away. Now, with a swift movement, he was at the door, which he jerked open. A man stood there sallow-faced, wearing a waiter's clothes. He smirked and attempted to appear as if he wasn't particularly taken aback.

'You rang, sir?'

'You need your hearing fixing.' Hammond rasped. 'Try some other room.'

He shut the door and turned back to Johnny Austin, raising an eyebrow at him, questioningly. The other shook his head. 'Never seen him before. Besides why should I want him eavesdropping? I can do my own listening.'

A growing uneasiness gripped Mike Hammond. Things were mounting to a crescendo. He could feel it in his bones. The pressure of the Smith and Wesson in the built-in holster inside his jacket made a comforting feeling. He dragged at his cigarette.

'You were saying,' he murmured to Johnny Austin, 'how you're the Comte's confidential secretary?'

'So I knew things. I knew about the girl, Ruth Stratton.'

Hammond's gaze narrowed bleakly. 'You know who murdered her last night?'

The other went ashen-faced. 'So that's what happened.'

He seemed to sag physically, as he went on hoarsely: 'Theo Powell did it. He had no choice, I suppose. Even though she knew nothing — oh, she and the Comte, they'd had this brief affair. But she knew nothing about what was going on. Only Powell must have been scared she'd find out.'

'Where would Raoul Dulane figure in this?'

'He knew everything.' Austin's head came up. 'You don't mean that he — ?'

Mike Hammond nodded. 'Stabbed to death,' he said. 'You think Powell took care of him, too?'

The eyes behind the horn-rims were

glazed with horror. The scar was a thin livid weal. 'When — when was this?' he gasped.

'Last night, also. Which is why I'm asking about Powell. He was around quite a bit. He'd have taken care of me if I hadn't done it first.'

Austin nodded. 'And now, he — '

'He'd served his turn,' Hammond said, stubbing out his cigarette.

Suddenly Johnny Austin was on his feet, his face contorted, his fingers clutching at his blond head, in a paroxysm of anguished horror.

'The monster,' he grated between his teeth. 'The damned monster — the blood of three people on her evil hands — '

Mike Hammond was staring at him as if he hadn't heard him correctly.

'Her hands?' he rasped. 'Who — ?'

'Faith Dulane,' the other snarled at him, as if it was being dragged from his throat by force. 'Didn't you realise — ? She was blackmailing him, her own husband. She had grown to hate him. She meant to ruin him, to smash him — '

He was incoherent for several moments.

Then he pulled himself together, and Mike Hammond, his grey-ice eyes narrowed, listened to him as he blurted out his story of how he had become Faith Dulane's lover, usurping Theo Powell.

Powell had been deliberately used by her to act as the blackmailing go-between, after she had discovered her husband's indiscretion with Ruth Stratton.

Austin pictured Faith Dulane as a twisted psychotic, growing increasingly obsessed with encompassing her utterly unsuspecting husband's destruction, his career, socially and financially.

As the other poured out his account of her perverted evil, a living, breathing destroying malevolence, Hammond needed to be no psychiatrist to be convinced that this was the brain behind the blackmail plot and the murders. His mind flashed back to the boathouse, where he had found Faith, apparently half-dead by hanging.

He told the other about it.

'A typical trick of hers,' Austin explained. 'She knew you meant to root out the blackmailer and she was going to stop you. She was tough and implacable and she was determined to grab your sympathy, while at the same time turn your suspicion on the Comte. What better way than the way she acted that for you? Then you were supposed to have fallen for her . . .'

Mike Hammond recalled the beauty of that pale face, the allure of her scented form in his arms. Johnny Austin's mouth thinned grimly. 'They all fell for her,' he said. 'And she destroyed them all.'

He went on hurriedly, confusedly, but the essentials were easy to grasp.

The murder of Raoul Dulane and Ruth Stratton had been committed by Theo Powell at her instigation; then she had eliminated him, planting his body in Mike Hammond's car with the object of implicating him.

'She didn't miss much,' Johnny Austin said. 'She could have the police breathing down your neck any minute now.'

Mike Hammond formed a mental picture of her façade of helpless loveliness, behind which she would scheme and act with deadly effect. He suddenly thought of her alone with her husband at The Turrets.

It was as if Austin had caught the sudden drift of his apprehension.

'She'd have the way clear to wipe out her husband — ' he started to say. Then Hammond heard purposeful footsteps outside in the passage. With a swift movement he snapped the key in the lock. It was a flimsy door and he turned to the other, who gave a nod at the window.

It was the way he'd got in, he explained. He'd wanted it to be a surprise. Along a sloping roof, it was a short drop to the garage-yard.

Mike Hammond was at the window, every bit of him galvanised with a new urgency. Then there came a sudden rap at the door followed by a voice. 'Mr. Hammond, are you there? Let us in, we're police officers.'

'Do your best to hold them,' Hammond told Johnny Austin, 'while I make tracks for The Turrets.' The other nodded quickly. The window opened, Hammond turned and gave a twisted smile. 'That expensive sports car; where did you get it?'

'The wages of sin,' Johnny Austin said,

and threw him the car keys.

Mike Hammond was sliding down the roof in the darkness, followed by the sound of the voices outside his door raised imperatively. He dropped lightly like a cat into the garage-yard of the pub and saw the sports job, gleaming white under a single electric light, where Austin had parked it.

As he reached it, a huge figure loomed up out of the shadows; a policeman on guard.

The policeman grunted menacingly. As this was no time for explanations, Hammond shifted aside and let him have it, a judo-blow. The policeman pitched forward on his face and Hammond was at the wheel of the car, zooming out of the yard and roaring down the street.

Soon the headlights were blazing at the tall, iron gates of The Turrets. As he swept through them, Mike Hammond wondered anxiously if Faith Dulane had left.

Scowling to himself he glimpsed the lighted French windows overlooking the terrace this side of the dark house. The car squealed to a grinding halt. He jumped out, noticed another car parked by the wide steps and raced up them.

He gained the French windows to freeze for a fraction of a second, Faith Dulane held a sporting gun pointed at her husband.

Hammond smashed the window pane with his sleeve-protected elbow, undid the catch and was in the room as the woman grated at Comte Charles Dulane: 'So you were outside the boathouse? You heard —?'

'I heard what you told him,' the other answered wearily. 'That I'd tried to murder you — '

'All right,' Mike Hammond cut in. 'I'll take over.' The woman was already wheeling round on him, her face no longer fabulously lovely, but a demonical mask of hate,

'Put that gun down,' he rapped at her. 'It might go off — '

Her tall, slim figure swelled with pent-up murderous ferocity. Hammond's Smith and Wesson appeared in his hand and barked all in the same action.

A double explosion shook the room, followed by the woman's blood-curdling scream and the shattering of glass above Hammond's head where the gun-shot had smashed the french window in.

Blood pouring from her crippled hand, Faith Dulane, writhing like some wounded animal, tore from the room, her dreadful cries filling the hall.

Comte Charles Dulane shouted something, and the desperate entreaty in his voice held Hammond back momentarily. Then he was racing through the shattered French windows out on to the terrace.

Plunging down the steps, he heard the roar of Faith Dulane's car, which had been parked at the side of the house, and he saw it tear towards the gates. He dashed to his own car, as he caught the flash of other cars' headlights and sirens in the narrow road beyond. Police cars from Marlow, tailing him to The Turrets, he told himself, He jumped into the sports car, swung it round, and accelerated after Faith Dulane.

She was approaching the gates, 50 yards ahead, tearing for the main road. Faith Dulane didn't slow down, but was determined to make a left-angle turn out of the gates — impossible if she had the use of both her hands, let alone only one. Hammond left his car and ran towards the gates. The overhanging trees and the black sky were lit up by the approaching headlights. Hammond ran quickly — not that he could have done a damn thing about it.

Sick to the stomach, he heard a screech of brakes, but the crazed woman was travelling much too fast. There was a tremendous crash, as she attempted to turn, but hit the side gate, and as the car seemed to climb up it, it burst into flames. The darkness filled with an enormous flash — then the police cars screeched to a stop, hurrying uniformed figures appeared in the hellish light.

Hammond reached the scene to see the creature at the wheel of her car, a human torch. Suddenly, as if she knew he was there, she turned her face to him. Against the pillar of flame that almost engulfed her, her mouth was black, twisted with entreaty; her eyes sought his in pitiful appeal.

Mike Hammond understood the mute,

agonizing entreaty in her look. In answer he fisted the Smith and Wesson swiftly from under his armpit and shot Faith Dulane between the eyes.

'Best thing you could have done,' a uniformed figure at his side muttered. 'You couldn't have done anything else.'

'I'd have done it for a dog,' Hammond said, and then he turned away.

He walked back slowly to his car to the accompanying hiss of fire extinguishers used too late and sharp commands filling the acrid air. He could see the time by his wristwatch in the glare.

It was 7.38. All he needed was just about the stiffest drink in the world, Mike Hammond told himself, before he telephoned the office off Whitehall where his assignment started and reported that the job was done with.

2

TWO FLOORS UP, IN CHINATOWN

1

On the door's glass panel was: *Joe Rayburn, Private Detective.*

Rayburn was on the phone to Doris Adams, his part-time secretary, and 'legman'. There was nothing, he was saying. Then this expensive-looking woman came in.

'Ring me back,' he said. 'There may be some small matter.'

What a dump, she thought, looking the office over. She pulled a rickety chair nearer the desk, and sat down. She had nice, slim legs.

He waited for her to utter.

She hesitated. He wasn't sure if it was because she was nervous, or she was making up her mind to go or stay.

'I believe my husband's being unfaithful to me,' she said. 'I want you to find out who with.'

He took out a packet of cigarettes.

'Low tar?'

She shook her head. He put a flame to

his, and took a deep drag on it. He got a half-full bottle of Scotch out of a filing cabinet. He took two glasses from a drawer in the desk.

'You use this paint?'

'No thanks.'

He exhaled a stream of smoke, and dealt himself a good slug of whisky. She watched him. He had a craggy, lived-in face. His eyes were grey and hard. He returned the bottle, sat down again, knocked back a big gulp of the stuff, and pulled a notepad to him. He picked up a biro.

Her name, address, phone, etc.?

Mrs. Claire Vincent, Flat 20, Curzon Place, Curzon Street. She was living with her husband, Hugh Vincent. He was partner in the Berkeley Square estate agents.

John Markham, she went on was their solicitor, and a good friend. He had said to her: 'Damned sorry about this, I love you both. As for hiring a private detective well . . . Give him a little time, Claire. A month, or so? I'm sure old Hugh will be able to explain everything . . .'

'He didn't put you on to me,' Rayburn said. 'Who did?'

She hesitated. Didn't say that when she'd told Ricky, how Markham wouldn't buy the private detective idea, Ricky'd said why didn't she hire one of her own? She said to Rayburn:

'A friend.'

He didn't push it.

Ricky Jerome had been in yesterday afternoon. He'd set up this meeting with Mrs. Vincent. Her husband's loaded, he'd told Rayburn. And the bitch means to take him to the cleaners.

Ricky had told her how he'd lunched at Wu Fat's the other day, and Chinatown was full of private eyes. This morning he'd taken her along to an office block on the corner of Gerrard Street and Frith. Past all those almond-eyed, yellow faces, past acupuncture clinics; Arts of War and Iron Palm bookshops; a blue cinema, Wu Fat's, and takeaways.

The board at the entrance listed the Black Mask Agency; Missing Persons agencies; Skip-Tracings, Personal & Property Protection agencies; Etc. Joe Rayburn, Private Detective, was second floor up.

See him alone, Ricky had said. He

would wait for her.

Rayburn had stopped taking divorce. It was nothing like as lucrative as freelancing for Home Office special departments; Customs narcotics, or Central CID undercover cowboys. But this could be different.

'Does he know you suspect him?' he asked her.

'I've accused him of being unfaithful — he denies it, naturally.'

'Naturally. Wouldn't you?'

He watched a small muscle flicker at the corner of her mouth.

She was thinking she would have to be careful over Ricky.

'Any idea who she is?'

'If I did, I wouldn't be needing you. I'd have murdered the bitch.'

A slight nod of understanding, even approval, from him.

'But your husband? You won't want to murder him?'

She just gave him a cold stare.

He said: 'Has he got any hang-ups? Your husband?'

'Like what?'

'Like turning homosexual?'

Two small lines showed above her nose in a frown of distaste.

She said: no way.

He put down his biro. He finished his drink. She noticed his fingernails were clean. It gave her a bit of a lift; she began to feel more confidence in him.

He charged £100 a twenty-hour day. A week in advance. He didn't touch a case for less than a week. Payments for information received, bribes to servants, house porters, etc., extra. She would receive a daily written report. Mailed her, or she could call and collect. Or phone in during office-hours, 9 o'clock to 5.30. Hour off for lunch.

He watched her make out a cheque.

Oh, he asked her, casually: when did she first suspect her husband? Several months back, she answered. What started her feeling suspicious? He was being late at the office more often. Then he began having to go away weekends. Business, of course.

After she'd gone, he phoned Ed McNeill.

Ex-West End CID Dirty Tricks Department, Ed nowadays played it solo. He'd have the gear, and check out with Doris Adams, he promised. No problem.

She was the wife of a Central CID ex-detective inspector. During a getaway car shoot-out, both his knees had been taken out by a sawn-off shot-gun. With him a permanently sick no-hoper, Doris had gone and sleuthed at an Oxford Street store. She also did Dirty Tricks jobs for Rayburn.

He phoned her to meet him at the Half Moon.

He had done some homework on Ricky Jerome. A luxury pad in Cheyne Row. Had earned his bread as a pusher, but the syndicate was taking over, fast. Solos were being rubbed out like pencil-marks. He'd had to look for a safer line.

Like Claire Vincent.

At the Half Moon, Rayburn put Doris Adams in the picture. He wanted to know if she had any ideas.

It turned her on, the way he always asked her for advice. He was a loner, but he gave work to ex-cons he could trust, grassers, herself. He framed his own rules. 'I sleep when my nut hits the pillow,' he'd tell her. 'I don't need no pills. I don't suffer no bad dreams.'

She had worked with Ed McNeill before. He was okay, she said. Right on the job.

When he got back to his office, Ricky Jerome was waiting. 'Look, I'm a pal of her husband. I wouldn't like him to have egg on his face.'

Rayburn said:

'You're nobody's pal but your bloody own. What's the new scenario?'

He hesitated, then blurted it out:

'Look, I'll level with you. Okay?'

'Feel free.'

Jerome took a cigarette from him. He lit it with a gold Asprey job. He said:

'I want their marriage should hold together, like I want a hole in the head. Okay? But, a divorce, she collects a bundle, and I grab me a piece of the action. A fat piece. I told you, she'll take him for all he's got — this tastes terrible.'

He put his heel on the cigarette. He lit one of his own from a slim case, which matched the lighter.

'You mean,' Rayburn said, 'if he turns out innocent like a new-born babe, you want me to frame him?'

Jerome eyed him with admiration.

'I do believe you're reading me, sweetheart, I really do.' And he'd cut him in for five grand.

They shook hands on it.

Later, Detective Chief Super Greggson, from the Chelsea cop-shop looked in. He was operational boss on the Ice-Pick Murders. Three girls gruesomely slain with an ice-pick during the past two months. Details always the same. Ice-pick, and the killer, thought to be a male, a sex-maniac. At least, that's what it looked like. Question: But was that what it was intended to look like, as a syndicate put-off?

The girls had worked the Chelsea clubs and discos. They had been pushers.

Greggson didn't buy it, totally. It could still be a psycho. There were enough around. Kinks, with violent hang-ups, weirdies and freak-outs, you wouldn't credit.

He and Rayburn had worked together

before. Joe Rayburn roomed in Smith Square. He knew the King's Road bars and clubs, joints and dives. Knew the pushers and pimps, porn-merchants, hookers and perverts. He knew those you could buy, and no one you couldn't.

'The buzz on the Ice-Pick job is pretty thin on the ground,' Greggson was saying.

They turned the half-empty bottle of Scotch into a dead man, and kicked some theories around. Nothing sensational came up. Rayburn asked what did he have on his blotter about Ricky Jerome? Like he had no form, but Rayburn knew Greggson was deep into phone-taps and bugs, no matter how the top brass said you mustn't.

The cop started to say something, when Mrs. Vincent phoned.

'His secretary's just phoned he has a business appointment this evening. Won't be back for dins.' She sounded dead acid. She expected the works on her husband, where he had gone, who was the bloody bit he'd gone to.

Rayburn promised her everything was under control.

Greggson had caught her name.

'Same Mrs. Vincent who lives in Curzon Street?'

He made it seem casual. But Rayburn saw he'd started to sweat at the hairline. What interest had he got in Mrs. Vincent? Did he know she was tied in with Ricky Jerome, and with who else? He tucked the thought at the back of his mind.

He said:

'She's hired me to check her husband out.'

'Thought you didn't touch that stuff any more?'

Rayburn thought he could mind his own business. Greggson said: 'Know who the girl friend is?'

'That's what I'm being paid to find out.'

After Greggson had gone, he remembered the cop hadn't answered his query about Ricky Jerome. He'd started to utter, then Mrs. Vincent had phoned. Was it on account of the mention of her he hadn't answered, or had it just been a slip of memory?

Doris Adams phoned in.

Hugh Vincent and another man had lunched at the Connaught Hotel. He often lunched there. With businessmen types. She would stay on the job until 5.30, then Ed McNeill would take over, with the van.

'Any buzz from your end?'

Rayburn gave her Mrs. Vincent's news. Wherever her husband went, Doris Adams said, she or Ed McNeill would be on his tail.

At 5.15 she came on again. From a call box, corner of Sloane Street and Cadogan Square. She had picked up Hugh Vincent leaving his Berkeley Square office, she had tailed him to Sloane Court, which was a luxury block. He was now in a flat on the first floor. It belonged to Melissa Lambert.

Hugh Vincent had been a regular at Melissa Lambert's flat the past six months. Two or three times a week. He would stay for about three hours. Weekends, lately, he stayed overnight. There were other men. One, her informant had told her, smelt like a cop. He hadn't been showing up, recently. There was another regular. Slim, fair-haired, aged 30ish, sharp dresser. Mohair suits, Italian shoes.

'Ricky Jerome.'

She said it figured.

She went on: She had called Ed McNeill, who'd made it fast. With van. He had got into the flat next door to Melissa Lambert's. The occupants were out. He had punched a bug through the wall of her bedroom adjoining.

Joe Rayburn said he would be right along. Ordinarily, he wouldn't give you a prayer for this intuition stuff. But Ricky Jerome?

The first floor flat, Sloane Court:

Melissa Lambert kept her eyes tight shut. It was easier that way to think of someone else.

She had met Hugh Vincent when she was looking for a flat. He'd found this one. 'It's for the two of us, darling.' She was the first since he'd married.

He was the first since her divorce, she'd lied.

He reached his climax. She faked hers. Now, she thought, for the guilty vibes bit. It was always like this with him. She held his head against her wonderful breasts. Relax, she told him. Relax. She still kept thinking of someone else. Now, he began chuntering on about Claire. The old routine. She played along.

'Perhaps she'll get run over by a bus, darling. Or,' for something to say to cheer him up, 'maybe the Ice-Pick Killer will catch up with her.'

She shouldn't have said it. He pulled away, wearing his stricken expression.

'Darling, I was only joking.'

She put his head where it had been before.

Now, for the next bit. The bit about if his wife found out, she'd have the shirt off his back. This was where she had to chat how she just couldn't bear for him to carry this guilt-load. They would have to split.

It set him off like he was berserk. It was pretty explosive, scarey. She must never say that, he whined. Never. He was on his knees to her.

'I'd take an o.d., I would,' he said, through set teeth.

'Wouldn't that just suit her? You know I won't leave you, darling. Something will happen. It must, if we hang on — '

The phone rang.

Ricky, phoning at this time? Her eyes fixed on Hugh, he mustn't hear.

'Hello?'

She was thankful he hadn't a loud voice.

'Sorry, wrong number.' She hung up. 'Sorry, darling, some idiot. Where were we?'

She could see he was ready to show her. She really turned him on. She wondered how he'd run up the wall, if he knew about Ricky. You couldn't tell if he'd blow his top, or what. He was sometimes sort of uptight,

While it was going on, she worried about Ricky phoning.

He'd never done it before at this time. He was supposed to believe she was out. The hairdressers, or whatever. She really was scared he'd check her out about Hugh Vincent.

She watched him, later, from her window. He passed a van on the corner, and turned into Sloane Square. He'd get a taxi, and dream up what to tell his wife. It was past seven.

She dialled a number.

Ricky's voice:

'Hi, darling.'

She was sorry she'd had to fake it was a wrong number.

What happened, she said, was she had a headache. She'd asked the manicurist to come round to her. She didn't want to talk to him in front of her, naturally.

He said he was sorry to have phoned. Only he had this feeling about her. Some sort of premonition something was wrong. That she'd been taken ill. He'd hurry over.

'To check your pulse,' he said.

'Oh, Doctor, I can hardly wait.'

She made it sound a kind of lascivious purr.

In the van, Ed McNeill and Rayburn. And Greggson had come along, 'for the ride,' he said. He had called at Rayburn's office to answer the question: what had he got on his blotter on Ricky Jerome?

Ed had given them some idea of what

he had on the tape so far. They hadn't turned in a bad show. But to him it had lacked that touch of sparkle. Especially on her part, he thought.

Now, Ricky and her were going with a bit more of a bang.

On the slowly spinning tape, her voice:

'Oh, that's it, darling . . . Yes, Yes . . . '

This is something more like it, Ed said. He thought they acted like they were never going to do it again. Rayburn noticed Greggson lick his lips. His forehead glistened in the gloom of the van. It vas torrid enough, but it didn't make Rayburn sweat. He reckoned the cop must have heard that sort of crap before. Was Greggson, himself, a bit of a kink? Hadn't there been some buzz about him?

If so, what to make of the stuff he'd told him about Ricky Jerome? Had he blown it up a bit? Had he got his knife into him?

He gave a few ideas a whirl round his brain, only half-listening to the tape.

Next morning:

The Melissa Lambert story broke in time to catch the midday editions of the evenings. They ran a picture of her.

Newscasters had broken in on the d.j. programmes about the same time. She had been found by the daily help. She had called the cops. Then passed out cold with shock.

Rayburn had a meeting with Claire Vincent at midday.

He had several minutes to admire her elegant flat, while she kept him waiting. He carried a small black case. He was looking at a news-seller in Curzon Street, when she came in.

'Coffee? No?'

She was hellish nervous.

'A drink, then?'

'Only when I can get it.'

She got him a Scotch.

He opened the black case, and switched on. She clasped her hands. The knuckles showed white. He played her the tape featuring Ricky Jerome and Melissa Lambert. It was all he needed to play her.

He thought she would flip her lid, blow her mind. She paced up and down in jerky steps. Her mouth opened and closed soundlessly.

'Oh, my God — ' She got some words out. 'Oh, my God — '

She stopped him less than halfway through.

He looked at her with surprise. 'It gets explicit as it goes along,' he said.

She had pretty good control, after all. She pulled herself together. But she couldn't pour him a drink. She had the shakes that bad. He looked after himself.

Tears streamed down her face. Her make-up was a mess. It didn't do anything for him, and she got to the point.

'What's the deal?' she said.

'The deal?'

'Come on, don't fool around? What's your price?'

'Oh, I see what you mean.'

She would employ him at £300 weekly for the next six months. It would be a legit service agreement. He had brought it along for her to sign. Plus a cheque for £1,000 in advance. No funny capers, and at the end of six months, the tape was all hers.

She signed.

He bought a paper from the man in Curzon Street, and read about Melissa Lambert.

His meeting with Hugh Vincent was after lunch. It was at his Berkeley Square office. It would be highly confidential stuff, he had told Vincent. He had managed to sound a little menacing, yet somehow reassuring,

He asked Vincent if he'd had a good lunch, and he replied that he had. Rayburn opened the black box, and switched on.

Hugh Vincent stood like stone, as he listened to the playback of himself of Melissa Lambert, less than halfway through was enough. He had been staring out of the window. Now, he turned and his face was a dirty grey.

What he said was:

'You don't think I had anything to do with her death? I didn't, you know. But if the police found out about this — ' He indicated the black case, and moved to his desk, as if to give him support. 'My wife, you see — '

Rayburn didn't show much interest in

that side of Vincent's problem. He offered him the same deal he'd offered his wife. He had not a thing to worry about, so long as he stuck to the deal. No fooling around.

'D'you know anything about who did it?' Hugh Vincent asked, as he signed.

'Only what I read in the paper,' Rayburn lied.

At 3.40, he stuck his finger on the doorbell of Ricky Jerome's flat in Cheyne Walk. Doris Adams had kept her eyes skinned since early that morning. Jerome hadn't left his flat. Rayburn still had the black case.

There was no answer to his ring. He pushed the letterbox flap open. He'd heard a noise. It was someone vomiting.

Rayburn went in. He got it out of Jerome that he had heard the Melissa Lambert story on the radio. He'd happened to switch on the lunchtime broadcast.

'What he must have done to her — ' he groaned through the towel.

'Who's this?'

'The Ice-Pick Killer — '

Rayburn stared at him. 'So what's your problem?'

They were lovers, Jerome choked. The last two years.

Rayburn filled his face with disbelief.

'But I thought you and Mrs. Vincent — '

Jerome started retching. He stumbled into the bathroom, and threw up again.

Rayburn followed him. He opened the black case and played back a section of the tape. Jerome stopped vomiting.

He hadn't thrown up again, when Rayburn left him. He was crouched on the bathroom floor. He'd started weeping once more.

Rayburn closed the front door quietly behind him.

Doris Adams had been minding the store. There'd been nothing. She had got through typing the reports. Rayburn phoned Greggson.

'Make it *The Pier*, upstairs,' he said. 'Like around seven.'

'In aid of what?'

'In aid of a tender steak, rare, and a bottle of Beaujolais. And a few thoughts we might kick around on the Sloane Court caper.'

A slight pause. He could almost hear the grey matter ticking over. Then, Greggson's voice:

'See you, then. *The Pier*. Seven.'

Doris Adams had gone. He made one phone-call.

He put a flame to a cigarette. He stood by the window. He looked down on the dark heads and yellow faces. He wasn't seeing them. He wasn't hearing the Chinatown chatter.

Other faces, other voices chased round his head. Like Claire Vincent's, and her husband's. Like Melissa Lambert's on the tape.

He opened the filing-cabinet. He remembered he and Greggson had killed the Scotch yesterday.

He called in at a pub on his way to *The Pier*. He saw the 6.30 newscast. There wasn't much international action, so the Sloane Court story led. But there was nothing he didn't know already.

The Pier overlooks the Chelsea Embankment at the bridge. It is run by an excop.

It's a favourite meet for ex-cons and the Law. The swell mobs and Scotland Yard's Heavy Mob use it, so do other plainclothesmen and Super-grasses. And the syndicate goons. Food and drink high-class, and cigars and cigarettes. All reputed to fall off the backs of lorries.

Rayburn and Greggson didn't make much with the chat at first. They worked on the steaks and wine. Then, over coffee and brandy, and their cigars going, Rayburn inquired:

'She cheated on you, too, didn't she? The same way she did on Ricky Jerome?'

Greggson's hairline showed beads of sweat. His eyes were like stones. He took his cigar out of his face. He said distinctly:

'You bastard, what's eating you?'

'I went to see him. He was throwing up all over. Out of his skull, he was, about Melissa Lambert being slashed to bits — this ice-pick nutter — '

'How in hell did he know — ?'

'They'd been lovers for some while — '
He broke off. Greggson was munching the end of his cigar. Rayburn went on:

'How did he know? I spoke to him about that. I said, 'Funny you should know how she died. No one else did, except one or two. The media weren't told — deliberately. Then I played him a bit of the tape — '

'Where in hell is he?'

Greggson shoved back the table. He was in a hurry.

'Cool it,' Rayburn told him. 'You said how he could get crazy jealous, lose his marbles. And how he'd tried suicide twice. So he threw a brainstorm last night. The ice-pick idea was clever, so you'd blame the other nut. Turns out, you didn't. So he tries an o.d. again. This time, it works. Before I quit the office, I phoned. The doc was there. Been working on him with the stomach pump. But no joy. This time, Ricky'd made it.

'Tape — ?' Greggson looked puzzled. 'What bit — ?'

'The stuff Ed McNeill got, after you and I had left. He hung about. In case something more came up. Conscientious, is our Ed — '

'And — ?'

'And . . . she'd had a busy day. She drops off. But he stays awake. She talks in her sleep. About Hugh Vincent.'

'Oh, Jesus — '

Greggson sagged in his chair.

After a few moments' groan, he looked up.

'Who grassed on me?'

Rayburn recalled the description given of him by Doris Adam's informant — he'd been the one who smelt like a cop. Information received, Rayburn told him. And he'd made an educated guess. Forget it, he said.

'I should bloody well think forget it,' Greggson said. Then: 'Why didn't Ed McNeill go to help her? All he worried about was getting it on his tape.'

Like he'd said, Rayburn told him, Ed McNeill is very conscientious. He was hired to do what he did. Not spoil it by interfering.

The Ice-Pick Murders are still on the Chief Detective Super's blotter. Unsolved.

3

CHINATOWN COWBOY

1

The car stopped by the trees halfway up Wix Lane. It's off the A604, ten miles from Harwich. The Dutch courier cut the headlights. He was alone. He was on time. He carried an untidy-looking parcel. It looked as if it was bundled up in old newspapers.

This was the drop.

He heard a car-door slam, and a man came out of the trees. The man was dabbing with his left hand at some scar-tissue. It was under his left eye. It was like it hadn't healed properly, and it bothered him. It was a nervous tic. His right hand was dug into the pocket of his long raincoat. It was a dry, clear night.

The courier had a thick accent. He sounded nervous.

'You are Mick Kaufmann?'

'Who the hell else, d'you think?' Then; 'Okay . . . Relax.'

He took the parcel. It was securely

taped and corded. The courier turned back to his car. He didn't make it. The long raincoat concealed a sawn-off shotgun.

The noise was muffled by the trees. The Dutchman's shoes scuffed up some dirt as he hit the ground. When the noise had faded, there was a whisper of wind in the trees. Then, the sound of a car going away.

The Wix Lane killing made the Dutch front pages. The London papers didn't do much about it. Rotterdam Customs knew the dead man. He'd been on his regular run for the Dutch connection. Rotterdam's investigating detectives worked as usual closely with Scotland Yard's Narcotics undercover cowboys.

And as usual, came up with zilch.

Three-and-a-half weeks after the Wix Lane job, Frankie Willard was in Wu Fat's. Finishing his lunch, he picked up his executive briefcase, and went along Gerrard Street. He pushed through the yellow-faced throng, past the acupuncture clinics, the Arts of War and Iron Palm shops, a blue cinema, and takeaways. He reached the corner office block, which is on Gerrard and Frith Street.

In the dump's dark entrance hall, the board lists Missing Persons' bureaux; the Black Mask Agency; Skip-Tracings, and Personal Property Protection agencies, etc. The office Frankie Willard wanted is on the second floor.

There's no lift. He went up the grimy brown linoleum-covered stairs. He went along the second floor, and came to the door with the frosted-glass panel. On it is: *Joe Rayburn, Private Detective*.

He went in.

Doris Adams was typing back from a tape. She was wearing earplugs. She didn't look up. The man with the craggy face stood at the window. He could hear the drift of noise from Chinatown. He was hanging on to a glass half full of Scotch.

Frankie Willard registered the couple of battered filing cabinets, rickety chairs, and Doris Adams' cheap little desk. Joe Rayburn's desk was a solid job, but cluttered with papers, ashtrays and two half-empty packs of cigarettes. A large map of London was pinned up behind the desk. The top right-hand corner had come adrift.

This would be Rayburn's front, the cheap private dick. For real, Willard knew, he was heavy into the Dirty Tricks departments. He operated for Customs' cowboys, the Home Office, and the CID's undercover spooks.

'Hi . . . Joe Rayburn?'

The man at the window smiled. Only it was more like a can-opener's gash into a soup can than a smile, He moved to his desk, and gave himself a repeat dose from the bottle. Then he returned it to the filing cabinet. Frankie Willard put his case flat on the desk rubble,

'Tod Kaufmann sent me — and his best regards,'

Tod Kaufmann had said he's the only eye in the Smoke you can trust. Which is on account of he's the only one who knows every bastard who's bent, and don't know anyone who isn't. Frankie held out his cigarette case,

Rayburn said:

'I use these. Low tar.'

116

He used a quiet voice. He moved quietly, He parked himself in a swivel chair. Frankie pulled up a chair for himself and straddled it.

'It's his son. You know — Mick. He's like his only son. He wants you to find him.'

Rayburn pulled a cigarette from a pack on his desk. He put a flame to it. He took a deep drag down into his stomach,

'He's got lost?'

'Not an utter from him for gone three weeks.'

The last time Rayburn had sighted Mick Kaufmann was at *Ruby's*. He wore a sharp blue mohair suit, and a Chinese girl close beside him. Rayburn knew her name was Sung Lee. He thought she looked kind of vulnerable. Sort of innocent. He thought Mick looked like he was hell-bent for the big time.

Frankie said:

'He's sweating the top line something's gone and happened to him.'

'Like what?'

'Like we all got enemies, I mean, he is his only son. And I'm here to tell you, blood's thicker than water.'

Rayburn exhaled a long spiral of smoke,

'Tod and tricky Mick? You're spreading it a bit heavy.'

Doris had stopped typing. He looked across at her. She was taking out her earplugs. He thought her face looked suddenly drawn. She looked edgy. Her husband had been a West End CID detective, who'd had both knees taken out in a gateway car shootout. Not such a hot pension — she'd needed to work. Bob Adams had known Rayburn, so she was working for him,

'Coffee?' he said.

She took her handbag. Frankie Willard stopped her with a five he'd peeled off a wad.

'Have it on me, Baby!'

'Drop dead,'

He watched her go out, slamming the door. His face had gone a cold grey. He put a smile back on it. He returned the note to the wad. He said:

'Which reminds me. Did I mention Tod's paying a grand? Five hundred now. Five more when you deliver.'

Rayburn said:

'For locating the where's-it-got-to-now of a million-and-half of hash? Pull the other one.'

Frankie thought: for Chrissake, how's he on to that? He said:

'You making some point?'

'Anyone who can scratch his ass and think at the same time, he knows the Dutchman was carrying hash.'

'Only Tod was in the nick at the time. Remember?'

A couple of months back, Tod Kaufmann had bought a coronary while 'being held for questioning'. The usual drug-trafficking charge. It was routine. So he is recuperating in hospital in Ashford Camp. Ex-military and top security. The con is guarded round-the-clock against any attempt to spring him. Tod was safe from any con within, or any outside enemy. From where he was sitting he had the UK hash-traffic right under his thumb. He wanted out like he wanted a hole in the head.

Joe Rayburn said:

'Anyhow, I've quit taking missing persons. Try the crooks upstairs.'

It wasn't going the way Frankie had planned. 'Okay, okay,' he said. 'Supposing — it's like a hypothetical question — Supposing he is expecting something gift-wrapped from R-dam? And supposing it's his only son's job to collect, and does? Only this bastard of an only, ever-loving son, takes off for an unknown which-way. Supposing?'

Rayburn finished the Scotch.

'Ten grand, and not a cent more,' He gave the briefcase a tap. It didn't contain samples, 'Five now. And like five when I deliver.'

Frankie hardly hesitated. 'So, I'm not the one to hang about.' He opened up. The case was jammed with the folding stuff, which Rayburn helped count. Then, he wanted Mick Kaufmann's address, when he was at home.

So, Frankie told him, no dice, he hadn't been seen around since whenever. It was flat 104, first floor, Avenue Towers. It is off the top of Shaftesbury Avenue. The Chinese girl? Rayburn wanted to know. Zilch, Frankie said. Chinese meat? Never even knew he was into that scene.

Then Joe Rayburn got it like a kick in the head,

The vibes he was getting sizzled round his skull like they'd caught fire. Frankie Willard was putting him on. So, which way was he trying to pull him? Back off from Avenue Towers? Or, get jogging to Avenue Towers?

He said:

'So, we're into Wednesday. Come Friday, and I'll be making with the buzz. You, phone in.'

At the door, Frankie said:

'You betting heavy on it? Like you truly will have the hard news Friday?'

'It's this mystic thing I have,' Rayburn told him.

Frankie Willard went out. He made a shadow on the frosted-glass. The shadow vanished. As he headed for the stairs, light footsteps came his way. He gave a dab at the scar-issue under his left eye. It was this nervous tic he had.

Rayburn found Avenue Towers on the map. Avenue Place would be about fifty yards away. It looked like Avenue Place would fit nicely.

He turned as the door opened, and Doris Adams fell in. She made a heap on the floor. He picked her up and sat her in a chair. She hung on to her handbag. There was a bruise on the side of her jaw. She moaned. Her eyes opened.

'What in hell hit you — a truck?'

She shook her head. It made her groan. She stopped doing that. He was pouring her a slug of Scotch. It made her choke. So she choked:

'Frankie Will — ouch — '

His face set like a stone. He held the whisky to her lips. She sipped away. It hurt her all the time, but she tried a smile. It didn't work. He felt her bruised jaw gently. There was nothing broken. Her teeth were okay. She did better with a smile, this time.

He helped her to her feet. She made it, shakily, to her desk. She fell into the chair. She opened her handbag and started to fix her face. There was a streak of blood on her sleeve. She tried to brush it away with her handkerchief. It turned red. He couldn't see any blood on her face.

122

'Hope I broke the bastard's nose,' she said. 'I grabbed his case, and scored.' She worked her mouth. It hurt her to talk, 'He's a psycho. He was in the shoot-up when Bob got his knees shot off,'

He wanted her to get home, take it easy.

'I should have kept my big mouth shut,' she said.

Look, he told her, he had some phone calls to make, then he'd close the store. He shoved some money into her hand. Get the hell out, and buy a taxi home. She didn't want to know. He told her she was an obstinate bitch. He gave her the phone calls to make, and went.

She called Ed McNeill.

She checked from the map where he was to set up. Joe would be in the flat by three, Ed McNeill said she sounded like she had a funny voice, but he got the picture. He would be on the job, on the dot. He said he was sorry about her jaw.

She got Selby at his Horse Guards Parade office. He was working late, he told her, so any time Rayburn wanted to take a peek at this or that, it would suit.

Detective Superintendent Burroughs had a private number. Seven o'clock, the St. Martin's hotel, where Rayburn had a room. Burroughs didn't say yes, he didn't say no. She said if anyone should be late, whoever was there first was to hang about.

When he stood outside flat 104, his watch said it was coming up to three. He hadn't asked around, chatted up the house porter. Nothing like that. He wanted to make the trip quiet. He stuck his finger on the bell-push. Then, there were these spots on the floor. He took his finger off the bell-push, and dabbed the spots. They were fresh blood.

He went back to work on the bell-push.

He got no joy. He rang some more. He usually gave it twenty seconds. If no reply, you could say they were either dead or out. Then he got in his own way.

A flicker of life in the door-viewer. He was being given the once-over.

The door opened as far as could be expected, what with it being security-chained. Her eyes were liquid black, and slanted. There were also dead suspicious.

He said:

'If he's into meditation, or some such, don't disturb him.' He pulled some papers from his pocket. 'Just let me in, and I'll leave these for him to sign.'

'Who are you?' It was a low, breathy voice.

'My name is Rayburn.' He glanced around. 'We don't want to be overheard, do we?'

Her eyes stayed suspicious. 'What you want?'

'I'm a chief officer at Ashford Camp,' he whispered. 'Mick's father is sick. A coronary — his heart's got hiccups. You get it? Nothing serious . . . But if it gets worse, then it could be. You can call me Joe.'

'He isn't in.'

'So he wants him to sign these — Sorry — '

He leaned in like his hearing wasn't too good. He was looking down the spout of a Magnum .38.

'You got it by the right end?'

'Try me.'

'It's the comedians who don't know the end of a Colt .22 from the other, worry me.'

'It's a Magnum .38.'

'So you know about shooters? Is it your hobby — ?'

'Give me the papers, I will ask Mick to sign them, when he comes in.'

He thought about it.

'Well, you see, on second thoughts you might learn something you'd rather not know. Or, look at it this way — Mick mightn't want you to know.'

Her eyes were uncertain. The gun wavered.

He thought he might be in. 'Or, look at it this way — I could phone the Assistant Governor, get his permission so I can leave these. It's just this red tape, you see.'

She hesitated. The dark eyes held his for a moment. They disappeared. She undid the security-chain.

Mick Kaufmann had quite a joint. If it was his. Spacious. Elegant furniture. An Oriental touch, like the bamboo screen. He thought he saw one of the off-white

126

double-doors move an inch. Could be a draught. He registered the large drinks tray. A lot of cut-glass and stuff. There was a bottle of malt whisky. She had put down the gun, where she could reach it fast. All the same, he didn't totally relax. There could still be a knife at his jugular.

So he was around, and so was the Chinese number.

'Or perhaps he may phone in?' he said.

She shrugged. 'Sometimes he will do it. It depends. You want some whisky?'

'Just a large one, and I'll tell you some lies.'

She sloshed him a good slug of the malt whisky. He told her no ice. No, don't you even show it the soda water. She sat on the edge of a divan. A heap of decorative cushions stacked back of her.

'You're Sung Lee, I saw you a moon or two back? *Ruby's?*'

She looked different from when he'd seen her there. It wasn't that long back, but she had caught on about this and that. Fast. You needed to keep with the tempo in this ballgame. She looked relaxed. There wasn't a flicker of a muscle on her face. It was a lovely face, a wonderfully smooth skin, like it was kind of transparent. Only you couldn't see into her mind. She was tapping the carpet with the toe of her foot,

'We don't dig *Ruby's* any more,' she said.

He looked for an ashtray. She gave him the hint of a smile. He wondered what was so funny. She explained it.

'I suppose you thought he might have left a stub? Then you would know he is here all the time.'

He said:

'He doesn't smoke.'

A pause. She wasn't going to leave it alone. Through pretty, shiny white teeth:

'The fuzz, I suppose, they keep a file? Mick Kaufmann. In the top right-hand corner: *Top Secret*. He doesn't smoke. Or, chew gum. How often he cleans his teeth. Who he sleeps with. How many times a night he can do it.'

He didn't say anything. His thoughts had taken a spin-off. Something about her that had niggled him. It hadn't had anything to do with her, now. It was concerned with something that had grabbed him that time in *Ruby's*. Like a news-item he had read. Or it had been mentioned to him. By Doris Adams? Burroughs? This Chinese girl being washed ashore on Tilbury mud-flats. Only she'd had her face blown off so bad, there wasn't much you could do about her ID. Except she was young, she had all her teeth, and there'd been hardly any dental work on them. It would be in her file. Selby would have a file on her. You didn't get washed up at Tilbury with no face for nothing. No way.

She had leaned forward to take the ashtray with his stub in it. Her breasts swelled out her dress. She wasn't wearing a bra.

'He is fussy. He doesn't like stubs lying around.'

And suddenly the vibes were good. A kind of warmth was working between them. He finished his drink. He looked at his watch, he scratched his chin, he told her it didn't look like Mick was going to show, and thinking it over, he'd decided he would call back. Only he would phone first. He wouldn't want to miss him a second time. No, he wouldn't leave the papers. After all, if something happened to them, and they got mislaid, he would be in dead trouble with the Assistant Governor, it would be more than his job was worth. Etcetera.

All this time the vibes were good.

Their hands touched as he made for the door — he wasn't rushing out, he was taking his time — and her fingers tangled with his. Her hand was warm and soft. She hadn't picked up the Magnum job. He was certain he heard the click of a door behind his back.

He didn't mention the spots of blood outside the door.

Ed McNeill had the van parked outside a callbox in Avenue Place.

His van was a nondescript sort of red colour. Two of you could stand up in it, if you kept your heads down. You could mistake it for a Post Office engineer's van.

Ed McNeill said:

'He came out of the bedroom as soon as you checked out. There was a bit of chat about you, then they started. He

130

had been waiting for you to shove off. Impatient sort, these kids are.'

A second tape started as he played back a section of the other tape.

Joe Rayburn remembered her tipping his cigarette-stub into the wastepaper basket. She had leaned forward, and he had known she wasn't wearing a bra.

'Oh, yes. Y-e-s . . . Yes . . . '

She sounded breathy, and urgent.

His voice: 'Make it with the verbals, Baby . . . '

'Oh, Frankie . . . Frankie . . . Ohh . . . '

'Gets good and down-to-earthy,' Ed McNeill muttered over the sounds coming off the tape. 'I thought you said she was Mick Kaufmann's girl.'

'You can't win them all,' Rayburn told him.

He was remembering her again at *Ruby's*. That vulnerable thing about her, that sort of innocence. And then that other business about the Chinese girl being washed up on the mud-flats off Tilbury.

Ed McNeill was saying:

'When he's through with this, he'll be into the post-coital chat.'

'Stick with it.' And Rayburn told him to

listen for anything sort of special about the way it was being put together.

He grabbed a taxi for Horse Guards Parade.

Selby's department of spooks is over the old stables. He was up to his eyeballs in bent surveillance. Bugging, phone-taps, mail interception material; photos, stills, blue film-clips filled the fat dossiers neatly shelved round his narrow, low-ceilinged office. You name practically whoever, Selby could refer you to their file.

Rayburn spent just under an hour in the musty office, smelling of old horse-manure, sweaty leather, and Selby's shag-tobacco. He knew where to look, and he worked fast. She'd done soft and hard porn modelling. There were stills, and clips from blue films (privately made); shots of her nude. Shots of her from Hong Kong, Singapore and Shanghai news-sheets, magazines; plus a mish-mash of material from Hong Kong Customs' and CID Narcotics' undercover agents.

And he found a thin bunch of clippings on the Chinese girl found on Tilbury mud-flats. They didn't tell him more than he knew already. But he remembered how he'd come by the story. It was the bent cop, Burroughs.

He found Burroughs three Scotches ahead of him in the back bar of the St Martin's Lane dump. He'd had a hard day. Joe Rayburn didn't inquire what at. He was too busy catching up with his elbow-lifting. He had a hunch it was going to be a long day's night for him.

They went into the dining room. They worked on steaks rare-to-medium, French fries, and killed a bottle of Beaujolais. They were into fanning the breeze over black coffee, brandy and cigars,

Rayburn let Burroughs fill him in.

Tod Kaufmann gets tip-off that his beloved only son's Chinese whore isn't a whore. She's, would you believe, a Hong Kong Narcotics agent. Working with our Customs' undercover comedians, Right? So, she gets washed up down-river. Right?

Right, Rayburn said. His mind was on the fat file in Selby's office. If Sung Lee was the faceless girl on the Tilbury mud, who was it at Avenue Towers? Unless . . . He was listening to Burroughs.

Which Mick takes umbrage at. Which makes Tod Kaufmann suss his ever-loving, only son is into a cock-up with Customs. Like taking out his own, ever-loving dad. What gets Daddy Kaufmann real uptight is this big deal with Rotterdam.

'Now you and me, we're human, and blood's thicker than water. But not thick enough when there's one-and-a-half million in the pipeline. Right? So, Mick finds himself deep down under this refuse dump, where they're doing land-reclamation off Woolwich.'

Where does Frankie Willard come into the frame?

Tod Kaufmann's hit man, Burroughs says, 'Sorted out Mick, and his Chinese girlfriend.'

Rayburn had this picture of Doris Adams falling into the office, her jaw bashed. Psycho bastard, she'd described him. So, he was just about due for his comeuppance, Rayburn said:

'Tod Kaufmann sends him to me to find Mick?'

'Not to give yourself a hernia on his account, you dig? But you could get lucky, and come up with the hash.' He was reading Joe Rayburn's mind: If he had come up with the stuff, he'd have got his head blown off. Frankie would have hung on to the stuff all to himself.

'You're so right,' Burroughs said.

Question-marks spun like a top round Rayburn's skull. Like Sung Lee. Out there in the mud, but, then, in good, healthy shape in Mick's pad at Avenue Towers. Only Frankie Willard's taken over the both of them. Which was why Frankie had wanted to pull him away from the flat.

He was handling it so it made sense, when Ed McNeill dropped in. He set up the gear in Rayburn's room. He told Joe he'd caught on how the Chinese had fed Frankie his lines. How he'd come in on his cue every time.

Burroughs kept butting in: 'You see . . . ?' as they listened to Frankie Willard spilling his guts. How he'd taken out the Dutchman. How he'd collected a million-and-a-half from the Californian connection. How it was nicely tucked away in a Zurich bank.

'What a con-artist,' Burroughs said.

'You could almost admire the creep. Pity he has to go.'

When Ed McNeill had gone Burroughs wanted to know why in hell he'd shacked up with the Chinese piece.

Rayburn knew he'd got it wrong. He kept his mouth tight. He knew she'd shacked up with Frankie. But let the bent bastard work out his own angles. He was on Tod Kaufmann's payroll. Which was why he'd shown tonight. To pick up any spin-offs of chat which Tod K. knew, but didn't want him to know.

Rayburn could see the wheels turning as Burroughs worked it over. So, it wasn't the Chinese he thought it was lying out there on the mud. So, it could have been some other poor bitch. He said: 'To us, all Chinese look alike, anyway. So Frankie had hit the wrong one.'

Joe Rayburn got a cigarette and put a flame to it. It saved him the trouble of saying anything.

'Of course,' Burroughs said. 'I got it — ' The veins stood out like snakes on his sweaty, red forehead.

'Something bothering you?'

A sudden uneasiness sent a chill round the back of Rayburn's neck.

'Only one-and-a-half million.' He grabbed Rayburn's shoulder. 'The Chinese girl's his nearest and dearest — you dig it? She bites his ear, and teases the number out of him. Like you heard him on the tape, afterwards. It's like being putty in her hands. You dig?

Rayburn dug, but didn't admit it. He didn't like the sound of what was coming next.

'So . . . ' The red face was wide with a grin. 'Some smartie son-of-a-bitch bites her ear, and teases it right out of her.'

'You're leading up to something.'

'You — you smart son-of-a-bitch.'

Rayburn treated himself to another brandy. Burroughs shook his head. He was driving. Rayburn asked what would Frankie Willard be doing all this time?

Meeting with a fatal accident. If Tod Kaufmann can do what he did to his own flesh-and-blood, you can have some idea what he'll do to that psycho bastard.

'Next question,' Rayburn said: 'What's in this for me?'

137

'Good question. But the answer's not so bad. Ten per cent of the action.'

Joe Rayburn didn't trouble to work out what ten per cent of a million-and-a-half added up to.

He said:

'I con the bank number out of her. You take it, and take off for Zurich?'

There was a slight pause, then Burroughs said: 'I read you — like an open book.'

'What you read is this: Why shouldn't I, personally, on my own little lonesome, take off to Zurich, and collect?' He gave Burroughs that can-opener smile. 'I'll tell you the answer before you do. Because you're bent, and you carry the clout to stop me making the first move.'

'Correction, you smart son-of-a-bitch. I would stop you . . . *Dead.*'

Joe Rayburn finished his brandy. He put a flame to a cigarette. Burroughs' eyes glinted in wrinkled folds of fat. He told Burroughs he had a deal. He went out with him to his Merc, parked round the corner. Some more back-slapping and hand-pumping. And Burroughs drove off.

Since he'd been operating undercover,

Rayburn slept easier of nights if he switched his home every few months. He used a cover name. He left no forwarding address. Burroughs was getting old, fat, tired, and wanted out. Pick up the Zurich moolah, and slope off to foreign parts. Rio, down Mexico way, Brazil, some comfy place, where one-and-a-half million could make you happy forever.

As his leg-man to and from Zurich, he knew what his pay-off would be. Ten per cent of the action? Ten per cent of nothing. A bullet where it did you most harm, and a grave like Mick Kaufmann's.

The old waiter yawned at him that a lady was waiting upstairs.

What sort of lady?

Chinese.

She was in his dressing gown. Her clothes were on the bedside chair. He'd thought his dressing gown looked ordinary. She made it look like it'd come from Sulka, Paris.

He knew she wasn't Sung Lee, he said, when she'd taken his cigarette-stub. Sung Lee's breasts had been pretty but small. Her file had confirmed it. (Yes, she said, she knew the stub was a bug. It was why she cued Frankie Willard like she had. The spots of blood outside the door? No she hadn't seen them. But someone had caught Frankie a bash on the nose).

'My name is Sung Pearl.' Her voice was soft and breathy, 'Her look-alike sister. You can call me Pearl.'

She'd made up most of Sung Lee's file. The stills, the porn, etcetera. The press-clippings, and the rest of it. It was her cover. She was Hong Kong Narcotic's top agent. Sung Lee had been mistaken for her. Sure, she'd taken this job to avenge her sister's murder.

She wanted him to know she'd faked it with Frankie Willard. He understood. It was all part of the ballgame. He wasn't hurrying over taking off his dressing gown. It was warm, and it would never feel the same.

'It will be something for you to remember me by,' she said.

Later. The million-and-a-half. It wasn't there any more in the Zurich bank. 'It is with your Customs. Except,' she said, 'ten per cent of the action. This is for me . . . which

I would like to go fifty-fifty with you.'

Her hands were warm . . . tender. He said: couldn't they talk about it later. And it made her warm and happy he didn't want to think about it, yet.

Okay, he told himself he would figure what five per cent of ten per cent of a million-and-a-half would add up to. But later would do.

His watch said a quarter-to-four when the phone woke him. It was from Ashford Camp. Tod Kaufmann had bought a fatal heart attack.

Joe Rayburn hung up.

So, you can't win them all the time. So, he would be making a move sooner than he'd thought. The phone hadn't bothered Sung Pearl. She was fast asleep. His dressing gown was where he'd put it, on the bedside chair.

'It will be something for you to remember me by.'

He touched her mouth very gently with his fingers. He thought she was sleeping. He kissed her softly. She stirred, but didn't wake. There was that alarm-bell ringing way back in his skull. He was thinking of Frankie Willard. And Burroughs. He would liked to have put her on a flight to Hong Kong, the sooner the quicker. Come to think he would have enjoyed the trip, himself.

He got a cigarette, and put a flame to it, and inhaled deep down into his guts. He wasn't going to sleep, it could bring some bad dreams.

4

CAT THIEF

1

First time Fred Ellis saw the white cat, it was only for a few seconds, then it was gone. Like a ghost, you might say, it being so white and all. He saw it through the railings of the garden in the square. Obviously, it had come from one of the houses in the square. But even though it had only been this brief flash, the white cat made him catch his breath — he could feel himself drooling at the thought of grabbing it and shoving it in his sack. He reckoned Bernie ought to cough up twice as much as usual for fur like this one.

He'd been smart enough to check the time by his watch when he'd seen it. Just gone ten o'clock. Next night, he'd be there, same time. He knew from experience people mostly put their cats out about the same time every night.

It was a late summer night, and Fred Ellis had been on his usual prowl. He was a cat thief. He averaged seven to ten cats a week, at up to a hundred pounds a time, cash, no questions asked by a certain Bernie Hollins, who ran a furrier's behind Paddington Station as a cover for his activities . . . His vivisectionist clients looked down their noses at thin, scraggy specimens, and your fur dealers, too, go for a healthy cat with a good amount of well-kept fur. Though it was your regular vivisectionists who were your most regular customer. Needed all the cats you could throw at them, they did. Never-ending, the demand is, with vivisectionists. But take the fur business, well, it had its ups and downs.

Fred made his cat-prowl nearly every night, covering in his travels every part of London — sometimes, if he had a hunch, he'd nip out to the suburbs, like Croydon, Wimbledon, or Streatham, in his little van. This is all the gear you need for this job. A little van, as inconspicuous as you could make it, and a strong sack or two, into which you shoved the mogs. So long as they had enough air to breathe, they were okay. They might yowl and fight

146

sometimes, but that didn't matter, so long as you brought 'em back alive. Bernie Hollins needed a dead cat like he needed a hole in the head.

But this white mog he'd spotted in this square just off Gloucester Place, it was a real beaut. Your better-class area usually supplied your better-class cat, so he was there all right, next time. He had a specially large sack with him for the white cat. And suddenly, there it was. In the light of one of the street lamps, it looked a gleaming, brilliant white. Made your eyes pop, it was that white, and it even looked bigger than the first time. It was then he had the funny feeling it was expecting him. But, as before, it was there for only a few moments before it vanished into the shadows.

He cursed to himself. He wondered what had made it take off like that. Then it reappeared a few yards further along the railings. It was a misty night, so perhaps because of the mist, it hadn't seen Fred. He approached it cautiously, his sack gripped tight in his left hand, held partly behind his back. He rounded the corner of the garden, and still it hadn't moved. Something told Fred his luck was going to be in. Stealthily he went forward, his rubber-soled shoes making no sound.

The cat saw him. But it didn't make off. It stood there, its thick, furry tail flicking to and fro. Its eyes glowed greenish gold. Fred could almost make himself believe it was purring. He was only a couple of yards away — this was the moment to pounce. But the cat turned and proceeded alongside the railings. Fred muttered a curse and followed. He meant to nab the thing tonight, and no blinkin' error. He could feel his heart starting to race and his mouth went dry.

Once more, it stopped. It glanced back at him, those wonderful eyes aglow in the beautiful white head. Fred kept going, still cautiously. Once again, he was a couple of yards from it. And again it moved on. Fred began to think it was playing some sort of follow-my-leader game with him. Well, he'd put a stop to that. His eyes slitted angrily, his mouth became a thin line. He wasn't going to allow some bloody cat to make a bloody fool out of him — But not to panic, relax — take it slow and easy.

148

'Hello, white cat,' he said softly. 'Come on, white moggy, we're pals, ain't we?'

Its pinkish-white ears twitched, then it turned and went on. Sometimes it seemed to merge into the mist. Fred kept after it without hurrying, calling to it in a soft, persuasive voice. 'Come on, whitey — come on now, let's be friends.'

So it went for about forty yards, till the gardens came to an end. Now, the white cat paused, then turned down a narrow cul-de-sac, which sloped to a small row of garages. Fred followed. It looked as if it was going to play right into his hands — if he could only get it into a corner, it was his.

His face under his cap was pale, strained with concentration. He was gritting his teeth as he followed the cat.

Halfway down the incline, it paused. It looked over its shoulder at Fred. Its eyes glowed with a greater intensity than ever. Fred drew nearer, talking cajolingly.

He saw that the half-door of the end garage to his left was slightly ajar. Then he realised the white mog was making for it. His heart leapt; he could have laughed out loud with triumph. Couldn't be better, the cat was running straight into a trap. Once inside the garage, it would be cornered and at Fred's mercy. He guessed the garage was empty, there wouldn't be a car in there, or the doors wouldn't be left open. It was empty, sure enough.

He followed the cat more quickly.

Yes, it was going into the garage — !

He stopped to watch the white cat slip inside the slightly open door then he dashed forward. As he'd expected, the garage was empty, no car the cat could shelter under. He was slamming the door behind him, groping for his torch in his pocket, which he always carried . . .

Dozens of pairs of cats' eyes glowed at him from the darkness. The garage was alive with the white ghostly shapes of cats, their eyes, greenish gold, blazing at him, Fred's whole body crawled with terror; he gulped with horror and turned away.

But before he could get out, the eyes sprang at him. He let out a frightful scream as the claws ripped and tore him to pieces. Yowling and spitting with venom, dozens of cats slashed claws at his face, tore at his neck . . .

At that moment, two cops who'd been on duty at a nearby embassy passed the top of the cul-de-sac. Fred's agonised shrieks reached them and they dashed to the garage. One pulled the door open, the other following him. Their torches blazed and one of them switched on the light.

In its glare, Fred Ellis lay sprawled on the floor, one hand grasping the sack, the other flung out as if to protect his face, contorted in a grimace of horror. One of the cops bent and felt his pulse, listened to his heart. He looked up, shaking his head. Fred was dead.

'What in hell was all that about?' the other asked.

The cop who'd checked Fred's heart shrugged and glanced around the empty garage. 'Must have had a heart attack — or something — '

He glanced again at the dead man. There wasn't a mark on him. Not a sign of cats' claws slashing and tearing Fred's face to pieces.

Not a mark.

5

THE BEETLE

1

Dear Reader — permit me to introduce myself and explain the *rôle* I came to play in *The Beetle* . . .

My name is Auguste Dupin.

Born of an old and illustrious family, I am, as a result of various accidents of misfortune during recent years, become reduced to such poverty, I am obliged to reside in a grotesquely time-eaten mansion — this desolate cul-de-sac, the *Rue Bizarre*, in a quiet part of the *Fauberg Saint-Germain*, and long deserted on account of it supposedly being haunted by some apparition, whom I have never yet encountered and about which I have never bothered to inquire. Courtesy of my creditors, however, I still enjoy a remnant of income derived from the family estate, by means of which and employing rigorous economy, I contrive to procure the necessities of life and have ceased to bestir myself about the glittering jewel of

Paris of lights and shadows, perfume and danger. I am no longer part of Fauberg Saint-Germain society, or the highly selective *Cercle de la Rue Royale*, or the ultra-snobbish *Jockey Club* . . . Books my only luxuries, which as is well-known in Paris, are easily and cheaply obtained . . . So it was, resulting from a meeting in an obscure *Rue Montmartre* library, the accident of our both being in search of the identical rare and remarkable volume to do with supernatural phenomena . . . brought me into the acquaintanceship of Dr. Reginald Lessiter, a visitor from London, who, himself, had become especially fascinated by those labyrinths of the Occult, of the Soul and Spirit, those realms of nervous disorders and psycho-analysis, as opposed to physical manifestations found in normal medical practice — matters upon which I myself seriously cogitate, and concerning which I continue to seek further knowledge. And, even more, Dr. Lessiter had been mesmerized by my accounts of certain *macabre* adventures in which I had been involved . . . *The Murders in the Rue*

Morgue, *The Purloined Letter* — and more lately, *The Mystery of Marie Roget* . . . Which, as he was pleased to phrase it, depicted remarkable features of my *cérébral capacité* and rationcinative powers.

All very flattering to one of my modest temperament, retiring as I am, to the extent of idiosyncrasy . . .

This time, however, as you will presently perceive, Dr Lessiter was to become more closely — more personally — involved in the case in question.

Which brings me to *Mademoiselle* Faith Carteret . . .

During a visit to London some eighteen months before — when he had most flatteringly described me as having achieved a high reputation as a consultant in the aforementioned Occult, solver of mysteries 'of the Mind and Soul' — Dr. Lessiter had introduced me to *Mademoiselle* Carteret . . . who during that occasion, directing most of her attention to me, had leaned forward, her grey eyes fixed intently upon me almost the entire time — which had begun to prove to be a source of some embarrassment — though Dr. Lessiter did not betray any feelings ... I do not believe he is of a jealous disposition. Little did I foresee, then, I was to meet *Mademoiselle* Carteret again — though, then, *une victime des circonstances totalement different tout autre.*

To come, then, to *The Case of The Beetle.* The following narrative has been cast in the third person where it concerns the strange events involving Dr. Lessiter personally — and which he later narrated to me — as well as an imagined dramatic reconstruction of the horrific experiences that befell poor Mademoiselle Faith Carteret, the real nature of which may never be fully known.

So it was, then:

I arrived at Victoria Railway Terminus this evening, and will break off here to allow Dr. Lessiter himself to unfold this extraordinary, not to say, *macabre* tale.

2

The front-doorbell rang and Lessiter called to Matthews, who was in the hall,

'Can't be the cab — ?'

'It is rather early, sir.'

'Wasn't expecting it for half-an-hour — ' Lessiter said, Matthews coming into the study, wearing a puzzled expression.

Matthews nodded, 'Seven o'clock, was what I said.'

The doorbell rang again, this time for a few seconds longer, and Lessiter scowled at his manservant, 'He's deuced impatient — '

'Yes, sir . . . '

Matthews turned back to the hall, Lessiter calling after him, 'You haven't helped me fix my tie — '

It was only a black tie occasion — he being due at one of Lady Bathurst's 'Little Evenings' at No. 5, that over-large house bulking twice as wide and high, squeezed between Nos. 4 and 6, Little

Cheyne Row — but Faith Carteret would be there — which would make it an occasion of enormous importance to him.

Especially, this evening:

More important than any other evening he'd been with her . . . just the two of them. Funny thing, he thought, you could be more alone with someone at a dance than you could be with just a handful of people around . . .

He never could tie his tie — ever since he'd been obliged to wear one, black or white, anyway.

Matthews was opening the front door.

A shadowed face beneath a black, wide-brimmed hat, framed against the quiet dark mist from Hyde Park, bent forward at him menacingly.

'Good evening, sir — Is Dr. Lessiter expecting you — ?'

'Say I have come.'

Even as he spoke, the other was in the hall, his voice raised impatiently. 'I have come a long journey — '

'Well — er — yes, sir . . . What — er — that is, what name — shall I say — ?'

The visitor was slamming the door shut

behind him, then Matthews found himself pushed into the study doorway, starting to say to Lessiter:

'It is a gentleman — '

'The cab — ?'

Matthews shook his head, and swallowed.

'What's the matter with you? And I want you to help me with this tie — '

'He forced his way in — he insists on — '

'What's going on — you're shaking all over — ?'

'He — he pushed past me — '

'Tell him to push off again — or you'll send for the police — '

'No one will send for the police — '

Now, the dark, menacing figure stood framed at the study door, hat pulled over his glittering eyes.

'Who the devil — ?'

Lessiter scowled at him, shaking his head in disbelief.

'You do not know me — ' The voice harshly sibilant, with a rough foreign accent — a sort of 'Eastern' accent.

'And I damn well don't want to — !'

Lessiter took a step forward, as if physically intending to throw the other out.

'Calm yourself, Doctor — '

Lessiter stopped and scowled at him — but now a little uncertainly. He wasn't used to being addressed as 'Doctor'; he had, in fact, given up his Harley Street practice . . . At the same time, there was such a horrific menace about the other's appearance, he began to think it was going to be a matter for the police.

'Calm myself — ! You impertinent ruffian . . . Matthews, telephone the police station — '

'Yes, sir — ' turning to go.

'We'll soon have you out on your ear. Now, make yourself scarce — '

'Do not touch me . . . I am a priest of the *Beetles of Isis* — '

'I don't give a damn if you're a — ' Suddenly breaking off, a hand to his head. 'I — I — the room's spinning round — '

He stepped back, as if he was about to fall, as Matthews returned, his face full of anxiety, and pushed the visitor aside.

'The telephone — ' he began, then saw Lessiter's hands to his face, and went quickly to him to support him — 'it's — it's — out of order — '

'You will be unable to use it, while I am here — ' the visitor rasped.

'We'll see about that . . . ' Lessiter, dropping his hands to stare at the other. 'Matthews, fetch a police officer — '

'Very well, sir.'

Matthews started somewhat uncertainly — it was a procedure he wasn't altogether familiar with — for the front door.

'You will not find him. There is a fog.'

'Fog — ?' from Lessiter.

'It will clear — when I have gone.'

'Open the window — ' Lessiter, glaring at the other, then turning to Matthews, who obeyed quickly, drawing back the heavy curtains and opening the side-window onto the street — only to immediately draw back, coughing.

'There *is* a fog, sir . . . Must have come up suddenly.'

'Then, close it.'

As Matthews promptly obeyed, closing

163

the window, Lessiter turned again to the intruder, 'Fancy yourself as a some — some ju-ju merchant, eh?'

'I am come from Ancient Egypt . . . '

'More likely from some music-hall — ! Well, now I don't wish to appear inhospitable — but the performance is over — and my cab's coming to take me to a quite different kind of entertainment.'

'You are expected at the grand house by the dark river,' the other responded.

A slight pause, as Lessiter stared at the other uncertainly, then:

'A clairvoyant — as well as a magician, eh — ? Well, since you mention it — I am, as you say, 'expected' . . . ' turning to Matthews, who stood anxiously at the door, 'Shout, when the cab's here — '

Matthews gave a nod, and went into the hall

'Faith Carteret . . . She will be there,' the visitor said, then, 'Continue tying your tie — you will want to appear your best — '

'If it's Miss Carteret you've come to talk about, you can save your breath.'

164

A pause, then, 'And Charles Atherton?'

The question was softly spoken, almost a whisper, and Lessiter turned from the study's mirror and his gaze narrowed at the dark, menacing intruder. What the devil was this all about? 'As for him — ' he responded shortly, 'I am even less interested in anything you may have to say.'

'Ah, yes. But — to you, *she* is all the world — '

Lessiter made no reply.

The other persisted. 'But *he* is bad — ah, he — there is something about *him* . . . of which you — of which you are afraid . . . '

Lessiter was attempting to make some connection between this weird creature's intrusion not only in his house — but in his life — his private life — what did he know about Faith . . . ? And, more disturbing — a trifle more disturbing — about Atherton? Charles Atherton, who had figured in his reckoning hardly noticeably, until more recently — and only then because he'd shown up on the scene at the same time, and the same occasion, as Faith.

It was at the *Society of Egypt* 'X' — the 'X' was to do with the Society being concerned with research into that particularly unknown chapter of Ancient Egyptian history — its rather 'weird' history — way back . . . way, way back, in fact. When there'd been a lot of quite horrific 'goings-on' to do with the Occult, etc . . . He'd agreed to speak — he'd become a bit of an 'authority' on the subject . . .

Yes, that was it, and Faith had been there — and on that particular occasion there'd been *Atherton* — *standing at the back*. Though he didn't recall seeing him afterwards. Had he been there on account of Faith? Now — the arrival of this — this creature, on the scene seemed to suggest there had been some — some connection between them — though it had never occurred to him before. Then, why should it have? He gave a sudden shiver, and ignoring his visitor, called,

'Matthews, where's that damned cab —?'

'It will not arrive until I say.'

Lessiter gave a start, as if of surprise the other was still there. A slight pause, then: 'What's your game?'

'And I am come to warn you . . . ' The strange sibilant speech was even more of a whisper, each word uttered with deadly emphasis. 'That is my 'game', as you put it. He is powerful, ruthless. She — ah, she — is gentle and sweet — '

'Look here — '

'Revenge is my 'game' . . . is what I am about. Revenge and destruction to he who has defiled our sacred temple — who has spat upon our altar — '

'Matthews — ' Lessiter, who wasn't listening to the other, again called out. 'Isn't that cab here?'

'*You* also will seek revenge,' the other went on, still that deadly whisper, 'When he has destroyed your happiness, crushed your love into the dust . . . '

Now the room seemed filled with a choking darkness — and where the intruder stood became something — some glinting, phosphorescent shape, with arms that began to beat as noiseless wings.

' . . . when you will cry out for me — and I shall answer in the name of the *Beetle of Isis*.'

'What's that? A beetle — a huge beetle!' Lessiter's voice rose in sudden horror. 'Ahh — !' Masking his face with his left arm, as Matthews came hurrying in, his face filled with concern,

There was a buzzing — like some kind of — of — insect —

'Didn't you see?' Lessiter cried, 'Turned into a monstrous beetle, he did — !'

They heard the front door slam . . .

'An enormous beetle,' Lessiter went on, half to himself — then to Matthews, 'For God's sake — let some fresh air in.'

Matthews obeyed, opening the window, and exclaiming, 'The fog, it's cleared.'

'Fog? Oh, yes — when he was here — ' drawing deep breaths. 'That's better.'

Matthews, anxiously, 'Can I get you something, sir?'

'I'm all right . . . ' Shuddering violently. 'Got the creeps, that's all.'

'A most unpleasant gentleman — '

'Changed into this huge beetle, I tell you — ' Lessiter broke off. 'I fancy I could do with a whisky — ' Matthews was already at the sideboard, where among the wine-decanters, a whisky-decanter and glasses glinted, 'A stiff one . . . '

A splash from a soda-syphon; Lessiter took the glass of whisky, and observing the other,

'You look as if you could do with one, yourself.'

Matthews shook his head. 'I won't indulge, sir.'

'Some sort of illusionist . . . or magician — ' Lessiter taking a good gulp of his drink, in an effort at rationalizing what he had witnessed. 'From 'Ancient Egypt'! From *Stoll's Music-Hall*, more likely! Or that show at the *Oriental Palace* — that chap who's travelled all over the East — performs those vanishing-tricks and reappears as an ape — or a crocodile — to packed houses . . . '

'Quite, sir — though I don't patronize music-halls, myself.'

'Beetle from Isis — lot of claptrap — ' Lessiter broke off, and took another drink, more slowly this time, and, to himself, 'Though, he knew about Faith Carteret . . . '

He turned to Matthews, whose smooth-shaven face was returning to its normal pinkness beneath the greying hair, 'I'll certainly get in touch with the police — telephone working, now?' finishing his drink.

'I haven't tried it . . . '

'Better see — '

Matthews went out into the hall.

'Probably just a temporary fault,' Lessiter called after him. 'Yes, speak to the police tomorrow, first thing . . . this kind of nonsense happening in the heart of London — '

'Perfectly all right now, sir,' Matthews was calling back.

'What?'

'The phone — '

Lessiter, to himself, 'That's what it was — some music-hall trick — '

The doorbell rang, and Matthews called, 'That will be the cab, sir.'

'Well, I tied my tie without any help, anyway,' Lessiter muttered. 'Want to appear your best he said — damned cheek. Get off to bed, Matthews — you need a good night's rest . . . '

He was hurrying out into the street, and the pool of light from the hall . . . 'Number 5, Little Cheyne Row, cabby.'

'Dear me — what a business,' Matthews muttered to himself, and was about to close the door, when:

'Good evening,' a voice — Matthews thought he could detect it had a French accent — reached him out of the darkness.

'Oh . . . oh, good evening . . . sir,' at the slim, shortish figure who loomed up at him.

'I hope I did not startle you — '

'I — I didn't see you, there in the dark.'

'That was Dr. Lessiter, was it not?'

'Er — yes, sir.'

'I was able to catch only a glimpse of him,' then a slight hesitation, and, 'I am a friend of his, from Paris. Auguste Dupin.'

Ah . . . Matthews felt he could congratulate himself . . . He had been right about the stranger's accent.

'Monsieur Dupin . . . Was he expecting you? I'm afraid the doctor has gone out for the evening, and may be late returning.'

A slight pause, then: 'A pity; he would have been quite pleased to see me . . . Well, then, I must find myself a cab . . . '

Matthews frowned at the visitor. Why should Dr. Lessiter be 'quite pleased' to see another stranger who had appeared out of the darkness? One for the night was enough, he thought, as he closed the door on the dark, mist-shadowed street . . . while the slim, shortish figure looked to the corner of the dark, mist-shadowed street, to stare in the direction Lessiter had taken.

3

The orchestra playing Vienna's latest popular waltz, *Destiny*, and Lessiter, sitting this one out with Faith Carteret, decided to take advantage of a diminuendo in the music and clear his throat and say to her:

'Would you — er — that is, would you — ?'

'Yes, of course, Reggie,' she responded. 'What are we waiting for — ?'

She started to get up, but he said quickly,

'No — no — ' And as Faith subsided, he waved a hand as if dismissing the music, and his face alight, said, 'What I meant was, would you care to — ? That is — ' and ended up with, 'Can I get you something — a glass of champagne?'

She shook her head, and he thought she had never looked so wonderful, her hair a pale golden glow in the carefully flattering lights of Lady Bathurst's intimate little ballroom.

'You look lovely — ' putting his thoughts into words. 'Lovelier than I've ever seen you — '

She smiled at him, and patted his hands, which were clasped tightly together, so the knuckles showed white.

'Perhaps, dear Reggie, it's because I feel happy — '

She broke off, he thought he saw another chance and face alight again, said,

'Because you're — well — because you're with me?'

A couple danced past, and Faith exclaimed,

'Such a charming dress that girl's wearing — '

It wasn't quite the response he'd been expecting — or been hoping for, so again he came in, quickly,

'What I wanted to say, was — please listen — '

'I'm listening, Reggie. You don't have to shout — '

'Why must they play such a noisy waltz? It isn't as if we're at some *palais-de-danse* . . . '

'Oh, it's one of my favorites. Wouldn't

174

you really like to dance — ?'

'Not now — you see, what I want to say is that — well — I'm — I mean, I've — '

The music grew louder, and another couple went past, both laughing.

'What did you say?' from Faith.

'I didn't say anything — but I want to say — well, I mean, I've loved you ever since I first met you. I want you to be my wife.'

There was a pause — Lessiter scowled as the orchestra seemed to blare out even more loudly.

But her reply was clear — it reached him beneath the music, so to speak.

'Reggie, dear, I'm so sorry . . . '

'Oh . . . '

'I'm — ' She hesitated, then went on: 'There — there's someone else.'

'Someone else?' He stared at her. 'You mean, you love another fellow?'

She nodded, 'Yes, Reggie.'

'I'd no idea, I never guessed.'

'Perhaps I may have been rather . . . well — secretive about it — I'm so sorry — '

He was staring at her — a disbelieving stare as, suddenly, he realized she was talking about Atherton — Atherton for God's sake! And his blood ran cold — Yes . . . That was the only way he could describe it.

'*He is bad — there is something about him, of which you are afraid . . .* '

What had that creature who'd burst in on him earlier been driving at — ? It was as if he had foreseen what Faith had just told him . . . Told him to his face, it was Atherton she was in love with . . . Charles Atherton — And he wanted to burst out with a warning — *that creature's warning against him* — To explain what had happened barely an hour since — but he dare not . . . That was the last thing he dare do — !

Anything he tried to say against Atherton would be bound to drive her closer to him.

Faith Carteret's eyes were shadowed with apprehension. As if she was only this minute beginning to realize the shock she'd give him — though she couldn't realize to what extent.

'Dear Reggie — ' she began, then broke off. 'Oh dear — I see Major Kimball coming over — ' She couldn't help it, but her tone brightened with relief at Kimball's approach. 'I promised him this dance, I — I think — '

And Lessiter himself could sense her lightening of heart at being presented with an excuse to . . . escape his offer — of his love — and any explanation, he thought bitterly, of why she had preferred the other to him . . . Getting up and fiddling with his tie — and at the same time managing to force a kind of grin to his lips, and unable to think of anything else to say, he contrived to come out with,

'Well — I think I'll . . . that is, I'll make myself scarce — ' And managed to add, '*Etcetera* . . . ' He couldn't force himself to offer her any congratulations!

'You're going?'

'I — I think I will . . . ' Putting his hands in his pockets and taking them out again. 'Good-night, Faith — That is — er — '

Suddenly, he found himself too stiff with apprehension, a sickening feeling in his gut — behind the fury he felt towards Atherton — and he headed quickly for the hall . . .

Behind him, Major Kimball was barging in between his departing form and Faith.

'You look positively blooming tonight, my dear. Like an exotic flower, if I may say so. Shall we . . . ?' He broke off, then, 'Suppose we'll soon be congratulating some happy fellow?'

'Congratulate?'

'Who you're in love with. Shall we — ' Again, holding out his hands to her. 'Isn't Reggie Lessiter, eh? Thought I saw him sloping off — but then, he'd be full of the joys of Spring — instead, he looked a trifle — er — outraged . . . By Jove, you're like dancing with a shadow — don't find an old soldier too heavy in the going — ?'

'Of course not — ' she replied. 'And as if we haven't danced before — '

The Major chuckled, feeling duly flattered. Then he broke off suddenly,

'Isn't that Charles Atherton — ?'

'Charles — ?' Her voice was sharp, suddenly. 'Where?'

'Good Lord — didn't know he showed up at affairs like this.'

'I — oh — ' A slight gasp. 'Would you please forgive me?'

'What?'

'I think Charles — Mr. Atherton — wants to speak to me.'

'I daresay so does every other man in the room — I was enjoying our dance — ' He broke off. 'I say, you've gone quite pale.'

'It's all right — ' She was suddenly staring. 'I — I thought I saw someone with Mr. Atherton . . . A figure — a dark figure — '

'You're trembling, my dear — '

'I — I'm all right — I — I must have been mistaken . . . ' She was already moving away, 'I do want a word with Mr. Atherton . . . '

The Major, mouth slightly open with surprise, watched her as she hurried off.

A few moments later, she was saying to the tall, heavy-shouldered man — who was holding out his hands to her,

'Charles.' It was more of a half-whisper — 'I — I thought you were in Cairo — '

179

'Oh, my love — it — it is your cousin ... There has been an accident — ' Atherton's left arm was round her shoulder — the heavy gold ring on his little finger of his left hand, shaped like a scarab — a beetle with a jet-black spot on either side — glittered as if it were alive.

His voice died away as he hurried her to the cab he'd kept waiting for her.

★   ★   ★

Some dozen minutes later, and they were drawing up outside the small house in Ebury Street, and instructing the cabbie to wait. Charles Atherton saw Faith to the front door.

She held out her key, 'My — my hand's shaking so — '

He turned the key in the lock and the door opened quietly. He didn't follow her into the hall. In the hall-light, her face was deathly pale. She turned back to him, 'I can't believe it's really happened ... '

'Don't mention it — not to say anything about — '

'No — no — I won't — of course

. . . Oh, my God — !'

'Just say you've suffered a migraine attack — You just want to rest — '

He took her arm and stood between her and the street as if to shield her from an attack from the darkness . . . And a thick-set figure in a heavy over-coat, hat pulled over his eyes, watched from the shadows of the next door house.

'Migraine attack . . . ' Faith nodded. 'Yes — that's what I'll say — '

'Do not hurry — '

She shook her head, 'Just a few things for the journey — '

She moved like an automaton — as if he was controlling her every thought, then broke off and tried to appear calm as Mrs. Allan appeared, her expression surprised, almost concerned,

'I wasn't expecting you back so soon . . . Good evening . . . ' with a little nod to Atherton.

'It's all right,' from Faith. 'I've come back earlier — ' She turned back to Atherton, as if for assurance from him all was well, he was protecting her.

He responded with a reassuring smile

. . . As he turned to the street, closing the door behind him, he heard her 'explaining' to Mrs. Allan, she'd had a migraine and just wanted to go to bed and try and sleep . . . glanced at the key he still held in his hand. She wouldn't be wanting the key again — he threw it into the gutter, and returned to the cab.

'Just a few minutes — ' he told the cabby.

'Yessir . . . '

'Then — Sloane Gardens.'

'Yessir . . . '

Atherton glanced up at the bedroom window — it had glowed suddenly through the darkness.

He was smiling to himself. A thin, self-satisfied smile . . . And his right hand clasped the heavy, brilliantly gold ring on his left little finger — it was shaped like a scarab — a beetle with a jet-black spot on either side, which glimmered as if it were alive in the gloom of the hansom. And there was as if there was a shadow behind him, which moved away into the darkness.

★ ★ ★

Some ten minutes passed, the bedroom-window had darkened and a few minutes later Faith Carteret came out, closing the front door quietly behind her . . . Atherton came quickly to take the small suitcase she carried, helping her into the hansom and they were off, out of Ebury Street . . .

As the watcher's shadow detached itself from the shadows of the next-door house into the pool of street-light — noting *Mademoiselle* Carteret wore a light raincoat over her dress and was hatless, her brilliant golden hair catching the rays of the hansom's headlamps, and carried a small suitcase, and she and *M'sieur* Atherton were heading for the dark house under the dark trees in Sloane Gardens.

He went and picked up the key *M'sieur* Atherton had thrown away and pocketed it.

4

Filled with a burning fury mixed with dismay, Lessiter had left No. 5, the big house between the two smaller ones, Little Cheyne Row, without the faintest idea where he was heading — now pausing to lean against the parapet, the mist-shrouded river sliding past below, its dark surface mirroring the flickering lights of Chelsea Embankment: No stars, no moon, only the white mist that moved now and then to reveal momentarily a black towering sky. A ship's siren from the Pool — then heavy footsteps approaching, and the policeman's conversational,

'Bit of a fog, tonight, sir . . . '

'Is there — ?' Lessiter not being much interested in the state of the weather . . .

'Comes in patches, it does, sir — off the river.'

'Does it — ?'

'Nothing — er — troubling you, sir . . . ?'

'Troubling me — ?'

'In a manner of speaking, sir . . . '

'Oh, no — nothing whatever — '

'The — er — the way you was leaning, sir — against the parapet — '

Without altering his position, Lessiter replied, 'I don't have to lean, if that's what you think. I can stand upright.'

'I wasn't insinuating you was the — er — worse for wear, sir — '

'Nor do I intend to chuck myself in, either.'

'I understand, sir . . . ' In a tone as if to suggest, that's what 'they' always say.

Lessiter stood upright and said, comprehendingly, 'I — er — I suppose you have a need to keep a look-out for suicides — ?'

'Some people being partial to it, sir — this time of night, especially along the Embankment.'

'Too cold and damp for me.'

'Yes, sir . . . '

'Now, a drop of prussic acid on the tip of the tongue . . . I'm a doctor — Good night.'

'Good night, sir . . . '

What a wonderful evening he was enjoying! Lessiter reflected as he walked on — turned down by the girl he loved — the only girl he'd ever loved, for some unknown stranger from the 'mysterious' East — or somewhere — plus nearly being arrested for being drunk! While Faith would at this moment be enjoying supper with aforementioned stranger at that exclusively smart restaurant at Claridges — *The Rendezvous*, wasn't it called — there was this thing, nowadays, about 'Frenchifying' everything in 'fashionable' London . . . At least a couple more restaurants had been 'copied' from Paris, run by French chefs brought over specially — that was right — his thoughts broke off, he stopped walking . . . That dotty visitor earlier on — ! Of course — that's what he was — a performer from that 'Frenchified' show at the Empire Music-Hall . . .

He walked on, keeping an eye open for a cab.

He was about to cross Tite Street, when a hansom pulled up at a house immediately opposite . . . A slim girl, accompanied by a young man, got out quickly, paid off the cabbie — and both stood silhouetted in the light from the hall, as the butler held the door open for them — Lessiter caught a glimpse of the girl's face, as she turned smiling at the young man beside her, and something caught at his throat . . .

For a moment he thought the young girl must be Faith — ! She had 'come back' to him . . .

She wanted to be with him, she'd always wanted to be with him, all the time . . .

He almost stepped forward, as if to cry out her name . . .

He caught at his dream. Laughed harshly aloud.

The door closed on the couple, to stare balefully at him across the street.

He let the hansom go, and for several moments, stood on the pavement-edge, his thoughts confused, the face of the girl continued to fill his vision. Then, continued on his walk . . . leaving his 'vision' and the darkness of the mist-shrouded river, behind.

Pausing on the corner of Tite Street, still without much knowledge of where in

Hell he was heading, a sudden flash hit him between the eyes — *That lunatic who'd barged in on him* — just as he was off to see Faith — he was having his usual trouble tying his tie — and Matthews rushing in about this chap all got up in some fancy-dress — and going on about 'What's-His-Name' — !

He'd known he was a doctor, as well — 'I am come from Ancient Egypt — !' He was a 'Priest' — or something — Then, he'd gone on about Faith . . . *And* Atherton . . . 'He is *Bad*' — (he'd sounded as if he'd spelt it with a capital B!) — Well, he was damned right he was *Bad* — !

And the 'sacred temple' rubbish . . . Spitting on the altar — Oh, my God — what dreadful nonsense . . . Then, it occurred to him, the 'Priest was on *his* side — hadn't he, '*Come to warn him*', warn him against Atherton — ? Or from — from Faith . . . From telling her he was in love with her — Because, this 'Priest' knew she was in love with Atherton — ?

Then, that 'Beetle' Thing buzzing around in the 'Fog', which had come up — all of a sudden . . . Some dotty Houdini

— or someone — one of these Illusionists — like they had at St. George's Hall — that's who it was —

Only . . . how did — *It* — know about him and Faith? He hadn't gone on about advertising he was in love with her . . .

Perhaps, if he had have done — he'd have done Atherton in the eye — ! Then . . . Come to think — and he was thinking — very hard . . . questions, inevitably, raising their heads, what did he know about Faith — what had he known about her?

He'd crossed over to Ormonde Street, still having little knowledge of where he was heading . . .

How long had he known her?

When had he and Faith first met?

A couple of years ago, he seemed to think — yes, at a garden-party that especially warm July of 1897, as usual, in Lady Bathurst's old Manor House Gardens along Cheyne Row — who'd given the dance he'd left only ten minutes or so ago — and a white cat had suddenly appeared, then vanished equally mysteriously, and someone said it was the ghost of young Queen Elizabeth who'd once planted mulberry trees there, ages ago . . .

He broke off, what the devil was he thinking about — his brain was a maelstrom of thoughts and ideas all about nothing . . . But, he went on . . . He had seen her once or twice at the theater, with a small crowd of friends. At a dinner-party or two . . . And, always, she was the same — her smile, faintly quizzical. That small corner of her left eyebrow that lifted very slightly.

'I don't recall,' he heard himself saying, 'ever meeting her at any 'do' with him — with Atherton.' Or, when he had been with her — he couldn't recall she'd ever mentioned him.

And as for Atherton himself — what did he know about him — what was there to know?

Damned little.

Couldn't be described as the typical 'man-about-town'. Didn't belong to any clubs, for example. None he, himself, belonged to — but, then, he wasn't much of a clubman himself, didn't play cards, wasn't much of a drinker — belonged to

The Welbeck — a doctor's club. But, infrequent visitor.

But, Atherton — ? Come to think, wasn't he mostly in Paris? Plus, hadn't he spent some time somewhere East — Egypt? Had some important contacts — 'Commercial' contacts . . . ? Probably, that was what it was. Or, could be a blessed figment of one's imagination — wait a minute — ! Thinking about Paris — of course,

Auguste Dupin . . .

Wasn't it when he — Dupin — was over from Paris?

A year — eighteen months — ago — ? Dupin had written him a note — a scribble, saying he was expecting to be in London, soon . . . Hadn't he mentioned it to Faith? Not because she'd be interested in Dupin's murder-cases, of course — but, because *she* knew Paris, quite well . . .

So, what was her connection with Atherton?

It stabbed him like a knife . . . They would have known each other, in Paris.

Now, he stopped — he wasn't quite sure where he was . . . The night had got blacker, the mist heavier, swirling around

— the starless sky showing itself at intervals. No moon.

He took a glance at his wristwatch — Ten-sixteen . . .

He'd been going round in circles . . . He seemed to recall turning back to Royal Hospital Road, and gone on towards Victoria — then turned off into a street he hadn't seen the name . . .

He'd left the river and the sounds of the river behind. He was beginning to feel on the chilly side. He shook his shoulders and pulled his evening-jacket collar round his ears — it felt quite damp . . .

A corner street-lamp's glimmering flame showed the name of the street he was in — Eaton Place. He shook his shoulders again and kept walking . . .

Shaking off Faith's sudden 'rejection' of his love — it was the unexpectedness of it — for that was what it amounted to, he had to tell himself . . . As if she'd decided that very evening — that very moment — only a few minutes before Atherton's appearance on the scene.

Yes, it was the unexpectedness of it.

He had ceased talking to himself aloud

. . . Had he, he suddenly thought, been flattering himself? Had he ever — at any time — really stood a chance?

Had it always been Atherton? All the time? Had he always been there, in the background?

If so, though, why had he waited so long?

Then a rotten, dreadful thought crossed his mind . . . Had she — had Faith — realized, known what he felt about her — all along? And waited for him to — to — well, propose to her — *to ask her to marry him* — ! For God's sake — he'd acted like a limp rag — as if Atherton was God Almighty — !

After all, he'd known her longer than Atherton had — he broke off — at least, that's what he believed . . . And no time — almost talking to himself aloud — had Faith ever realized the way he felt about her — never put his feelings '*to the test*' . . . ? Why not — ?

True, he'd never been much of — of a chap all that interested in — in falling in love . . . As a doctor, he'd practiced very little, had little to do with patients

— mostly when in hospital — he'd had
little to do with women doctors or nurses
— he had soon become caught up in
research . . . How the Mind worked
— which had drawn him increasingly into
'What Went On in the Mind' . . .

*Which was how he'd met Dupin
— Auguste Dupin.*

It had been quite by chance, some
couple of years or more earlier — he was
in the process of giving up his Harley
Street practice, concerned increasingly
with seeking re-interpretations of this new
psycho-analysis thing, plus, as he'd come
to believe — the important psychologi-
cally healing powers of ancient Ayurvedic
Medicine — and was in Paris, searching
for contributory information in an obscure
Rue Monmartre library, and encountered
Dupin, who was engaged in studying ancient
Eastern aspects of criminology, wasn't it
in connection with the Rue Morgue crime
horror?

Now, suddenly, he found himself
outside Atherton's house — God knows
how he'd got there . . .

Large place — tall, with dark trees

either side of it, as if guarding itself against visitors, the wind whispering through them — the whisper rising as he stood there, to a harsh whistle as it strengthened, then dropped.

A secret house.

The wide, black front door stared back at him . . . It had two large glass panels — they were shining black in the center, reflecting the night sky — and they glared back at him . . .

As if they were alive . . .

Then, suddenly Faith's face 'appeared' on the left glass panel — he pushed the gate open — started to make a move to call out to her — she looked so real.

She even seemed to stare back at him, and he was staring at her . . . She was looking as she had been at the dance, with the band playing that Destiny Waltz . . .

Then, the vision vanished.

The glass panels in the wide, black door were empty. He closed the gate and started to continue on his way . . . On his way, where to?

He suddenly felt desperately tired.

Whacked — that's what he was
. . . He'd take a cab — that's what he'd
do . . . Back to his house — should he call
at Faith's house on the way? He could
think of some excuse — Ask her
house-keeper, Mrs. Allan, if she was all
right — if she'd got back safely . . . ?

Then, he knew, of course — he
couldn't do that . . .

A cab appeared out of the night's
semi-darkness — was it empty?

He would take it. Still, undecided, all
the same he hailed it. Despite the heavy
gloom, the cabbie must have seen his
signal and slowed his cab to a stop.

'Number 12, Park Street, Mayfair — '
He could hardly get the words out, he
was that tired. 'Number 12 — '

A voice from inside the cab said — it
was a quiet voice, it had a foreign accent,

'Enjoying an evening-stroll, *M'sieu*
Lessiter — ?' The voice had a Parisian
accent.

'Oh, sorry — didn't see it was taken
— in the dark . . . ' he broke off,
'*Dupin* — !'

'*Peut etre* — surprised to see me — so

196

far from the Faubourg St. Germain?'
Lessiter could scarcely believe his eyes, as
he stared into the cab.

'*Auguste Dupin* — By all that's — ! Is
it really you — ? I — I was only thinking
of you a few minutes ago — '

'*C'est Destin* . . . M'sieu Lessiter — do
let me take you home — '

'*Mais non* — ' from Lessiter, 'Let me
take *you* home — where are you staying?'

'Ah . . . ' Slight pause, then . . . '*Le
Crescent Hotel* — '

'*Crescent* — Where the devil is that?'

'Ah — *mais oui* — I arrive Victoria
Station — it is — ah — behind it — '

''Behind Victoria — My God, we must
get you out of *that, vitement* — !' Getting
into the cab . . . 'You're staying *avec
mois* — !' To the cabby, '*Crescent Street*
— and hurry — !'

As they rattled off, Dupin murmured,
'You are very kind — it was short notice,
I hadn't time to write — '

'Knowing you, I doubt if you'd written
if you'd had a month of Sundays — !'

''A month of Sundays' . . . ?' Dupin
murmured to himself . . . '*Mais oui*

— *that* would be a long time . . . '

The cab turned into an ill-lit crescent of narrow houses, several with signs up indicating they were lodging-houses or unlicensed hotels, at the back of Victoria Station, and drew up at one with, across its front, *Crescen* — the 't' was missing — *Ho* — the 't' was also absent —

'Is this it?' There was a somewhat disbelieving note in Lessiter's tone.

'Er — yes — ' with a nod of the head.

'Ho-el? Looks more the sort of place you'd wake up to find yourself murdered — sooner we get you out of it, the better.'

'Wake up to find oneself murdered?' Dupin murmured to himself . . . 'Ah, a joke — ' And followed Lessiter, who went up to the reception desk and banged the bell.

'Shop . . . What a rat-hole . . . '

A somewhat soiled-looking individual in grubby, rolled-up shirtsleeves, appeared.

'Uh — ?'

'This gentleman booked a room this evening — '

'Uh?'

'I am *Monsieur Dupin* — I took a room.'

'Gent from Paree, uh?'

'Uh,' Lessiter responded.

'I am not staying, after all,' Dupin explained.

Lessiter adding, 'Come to collect his belongings.'

'Can't leave till you pays the bill — '

'Perhaps we could have it?'

'Uh . . . Let's see . . . ' Consulting a slip of paper — 'Won't charge for tomorrow's breakfast — '

'Most obliged,' Dupin smiled.

The other pushed the slip of paper to him, and he glanced at it. Lessiter asked him, had he any English money — Dupin nodded and pushed a note across to the man. Oh, thought Lessiter, come prepared for a bit of a stay — and wondered what it could be about — another *Murder in the Rue Morgue* case?

'I'll come up with you,' he said, as Dupin headed for the stairs; then couldn't resist asking in a low voice, 'Doesn't he remind you of someone you once knew?'

'That creature — ? Who?'

'The gorilla in the *Rue Morgue* . . . '

199

They reached the dimly gas-lit first floor, Dupin leading the way, Lessiter saying, 'Why the devil you didn't let me know you were coming to London — '

'This is the room,' Dupin, opening a door, and Lessiter made out the number.

'12a . . . Umm — '

The other glanced at him inquiringly.

'Used to be number 13,' Lessiter explained. 'Then something unlucky happened — suicide or worse — so they changed it . . . Take your bag, and let's go — '

'It has been opened,' Dupin said, without much surprise in his tone. '*Mon valise* . . . I do not possess anything of any value. Just things for the journey . . . they have not been taken.'

'How d'you know it's been opened?'

'The piece of black cotton I tied over the clasp is broken.'

'Umm — ? So you are on some mysterious business?'

'You said we would be having a talk . . . '

A trifle evasively, Lessiter thought, and, 'Come on — ' he responded, and they hurried down the grimly-shadowed stairs, out of the place, Dupin calling back to the man at the desk,

'Good night, *Monsieur.*'

'Uh . . . '

5

'I really can't believe it,' Lessiter was saying, some half-an-hour later. 'What are you doing in London — Not here on some — er — *enquéter de crime*? Such as,' with a little smile, 'another *Rue Morgue* affair?'

They were sitting comfortably at the study-table, the fireplace aglow with the brightly twinkling coals, the heavy curtains tightly drawn against the chill mist of the night . . . Lessiter himself had grown warmer — not only to the depths of his being, but his mind had calmed, his body-tension relaxed — such had been his reaction to Dupin's appearance on the scene.

'I had called here earlier, as it happened,' the other told him. Lessiter thought there was a note of urgency in his voice.

'This evening?'

'When you went off to Little Cheyne

Row. I followed you . . . '

'Why didn't you speak to me?'

'Er — forgive me . . . You appeared somewhat depressed in your manner — indecisive . . . ' Dupin chose his words slowly, as if anxious not to offend the other, who nodded; and there was a pause. Then:

'Rather a bad shock I'd had, as a matter of fact.'

'I regret to hear of it.'

'Tonight, you see, Faith Carteret, whom — well, I hoped to marry — when I — I proposed to her — after the second waltz, or it could have been the third — or, even the — '

He broke off — 'I'd wound myself up to it, you see — she checked me in my stride.' He went on, as if not realizing he was opening his very heart: ''So sorry,' she said . . . Or words to that effect — 'Only there's someone else'.'

Lessiter's eyes had narrowed, his features darkened. 'I mean, I'd no idea, never even guessed — ' He broke off. Then — 'I can feel it in my bones — there's something not — right about it — ' He broke off again, 'Good God — I'm chatting away as if *votre mon — mon directeur de mon conscience* — !'

The other smiled slightly. 'But I am flattered — by your *confidence* in me . . .'

'Why, it's like old times — Would you — er — be here on some murder — like that *Rue Morgue* affair?' Lessiter was at the sideboard, and turned to Dupin, 'Glass of wine?'

'*Merci*,' — without answering the other's question.

'Yes, it's been quite an evening,' Lessiter continued, pouring Dupin a glass of *Beaujolais*, which he took.

'*Bonne chance.*'

Lessiter nodded, 'It's wonderful luck to see you — !'

'The 'someone else' you mentioned — who is he?' Dupin asked, putting down his glass.

The question was quick — almost sharp.

Lessiter glanced at the other, a frown deepening his expression, 'Charles Atherton . . .' Then, 'You know him?'

'I? Why should I?'

'I — I thought you — you looked a bit — a bit as if the name — rang some sort of bell . . . ' He went on, with a desperate note rising in his voice, 'What can she see in him . . . ? I should have made my feelings — my love — for her, known long before this evening — ' He gave a sigh and muttered to himself . . . 'Should have had the courage of my convictions . . . ' then broke off. 'But I'm unutterably selfish, my dear Dupin — I haven't inquired after *your* circumstances. Still living in that ruin, No. 33 *Rue Dunôt*, that desolate cul-de-sac, off the *Faubourg St. Germain*?'

'At least,' Dupin nodded, 'courtesy of my creditors, the time-eaten ruin is still allowed me . . . '

'Scandalous! Someone with your illustrious name — '

'In Paris, these days, it is not so much one's illustrious name — but the francs in one's pocket . . . '

Lessiter nodded understandingly, 'London's become the same — everyone's money-mad.'

'Still, I contrive to procure for myself the necessities of life — tobacco and books — '

Dupin broke off as Matthews came in with a tray of cheese and lettuce sandwiches and biscuits, Lessiter indicating the place on the table at which Dupin was sitting — with a '*Merci,*' from the latter, and '*Je regretter ce que j'ai* — got you out of bed . . . '

'Quite all right, sir — ' delighted to have indicated he could understand French.

'Becoming used to unexpected visitors in the night — are we not?' from Lessiter, who then added, '*Monsieur* Dupin being a dashed sight more welcome than our last visitor, eh?'

'I'm sure, sir,' exchanging a kind of conspiratorial glance with Dupin — as if to remind him, they had already met that evening, then closed the door quietly behind him.

'An unexpected visitor — ?' Dupin, at the same time he was giving his attention to the sandwiches, queried.

Lessiter glanced at him with a sharp

nod, then his jaw set in a grim line, and pursing his lips, said,

'Well — yes — it was quite an alarming experience — had poor old Matthews shaking with fright, I tell you.' With a scowl of disbelief, 'This priest chap, actually mesmerized him — '

'*Priest?*'

Lessiter nodded, 'That's what I — I wanted to come to — ' Breaking off with a shudder — and taking a good drink of wine, he went on, 'Pushed his way in — he did — 'All the way from Ancient Egypt, I have come — '!'

'*The purpose* of this ... visitor, being — ?'

'That was what was so — so, well, disturbing ... '

Dupin was staring at him intently, then:

'*The purpose of his visit* ... Being to warn you, *Mademoiselle* Carteret was herself in love with — this — this *M'sieur* Atherton — ?'

Lessiter glanced at the other sharply, then, taking his time,

'Yes — well — it *was* about Faith and me — and — and him — Atherton

. . . This . . . this 'creature' — with a shudder — 'Ugh — ! He seemed to know quite a bit about him — more than I did — '

'What did he know about him?'

'Well — *he was ruthless*, and Faith was gentle — and went on about how I would be seeking revenge — !'

'On Atherton — because he had come between you and *Mademoiselle* Carteret?'

Lessiter nodded. 'Anyway, to clear off, I told him, and he — you won't believe this — he changed himself into this horrible beetle — '

'Metamorphosed into a *Beetle of Isis* . . . '

'Loathsome, monstrous, it was — ' breaking off to stare at the other — 'You mean you know about it — this — this?'

'The *Beetles of Isis* . . . Who were believed,' Dupin replied, 'to possess some supernatural *ruse* — some *ruse pour vous faire* — enabling them to transform themselves into a kind of half-animal-half-human shape — '

'Well anyhow . . . ' Lessiter went on, 'I

said, pretty sharply, you can bet — 'I
don't give a damn who you are — what
you are — !' Then this — this merchant
vanished . . . Matthews said he rushed
past him in the hall. Front-door slams
— and then, there's this *Beetle Thing*
— buzzing round, like the other one — '
He broke off, then, 'I know there was an
Egyptian conjurer — illusionist . . . Who
appeared at your *Theâtre des Variétés* . . . He
astonished — even mesmerized Paris audiences by the illusions he presented — people
appeared and disappeared at will . . . But
— I don't think this — this evening's
— was any music-hall performance — !'

'Sect of the *Temple of Isis* — ' from
Dupin.

'I expect you're right — you seem to
know about this sort of thing,' Lessiter
said. Then, 'Come to think — this chap
did seem to be *against* Atherton — I
mean, 'He is bad,' he said — warning me
against him . . . '

'Each may possess motives differing
from the other — jealousy — *par
example* . . . '

'When this Beetle Thing started up — '

shaking his head in puzzlement — 'Got the picture a bit cock-eyed — and can you wonder!'

'The 'picture' you have presented is as you perceived it at the time,' was Dupin's response. 'No doubt . . . there may be — *some* 'things' about it, which may remain — *inexplicable* . . . '

Lessiter nodded, then he was asking, 'How did *you* know this . . . this creature had been to me on about Faith — and Atherton?'

'You mean, that *M'sieu* Atherton had . . . taken your place?' A slight pause, 'As you may recall, I possess a certain facility in lip-reading . . . I had observed you when you left the house — glimpsed your face under the street-lamp. You were murmuring to yourself . . . '

'What an extraordinary *coincidence* — I can't believe it! You turning up at this very moment of my . . . of my life — '

''There are more things in Heaven and Earth',' quoted Dupin — '*Votre M'sieu William Shakespeare* . . . ' Then, 'What do you know about *M'sieu* Atherton?'

6

Lessiter picked up his glass, then put it down without taking a drink: *What did he know about M'sieu Atherton?* What was there to know about him Dupin might be interested in?

Auguste Dupin ... described in the Press the world over, as the Paris '*Detective*' — addicted, as one journalist put it, to conundrums as the opium-addict to the seed of the poppy — or the solving of mysteries of a supernatural kind, such as, *par example*, most recently, the horrific murder of the *Palais Royale* perfumerie assistant, the fair Marie Roget, by an unknown strangler — and, in whose mind, 'detection' meant a specialized way of unraveling a 'murder puzzle'.

Dupin's triumphant solution to the *Rue Morgue* horror — his original method of detection (never precisely explained to police or Press!) plus his use of the *nom, detective* — had transformed him into a 'household name' ... The *Marie Roget* murder, several months later, which had shocked all Paris, resulted in the Prefecture, who'd found the case insoluble, calling in Dupin — who proved the crime had been committed by a 'Society' surgeon, suffering from an 'emotional attack' — whose identity must never be revealed ... Dupin had deduced he had worn surgical-gloves, which left no fingerprints ... until he had examined them, *inside-out* ... But he had been sworn to secrecy.

What kind of 'conundrum,' or 'murder-puzzle' of a supernatural kind, did *Atherton* present to Dupin?

'He wears no neck-tie — ' he heard Dupin saying. 'It is a strong, powerful neck, bronzed by Egyptian suns — while some have expressed the opinion he has spent some time in *Montcalm* — '

Now, Lessiter was staring at the other sharply: '*Montcalm*' was a hospital for the 'mentally unbalanced' ... *the insane*.

'He is the son of the less stable-minded *Duc de Xancr*,' Dupin continued, 'notorious for playing practical jokes, which

212

often resulted in the victims' demise . . . '

Lessiter could only stare at him in sheer disbelief. 'And you — you mean, his name isn't Atherton — at all?'

The other shrugged. 'When in London, it is the name he prefers to go by. In Paris, however, or when traveling abroad . . . Cairo — further East, where he most often visits — he prefers 'Xancr'. They tell me, he has the capacity of — of physically changing into a large-sized beetle . . . but that may just be one of the many rumors in which Paris abounds. He is a creature of shadows . . . Now, he is there — now, he is not. They tell me,' he added, 'he is a steel-like opponent in a duel — has fought several at *'Maitre Jules' sale-d'armes* off the *'E'toile* — inscrutably-eyed he is, *avec* an impenetrable guard, full of tricks as any student of *L'Ecole Italia* . . . ' Adding, 'He may also be noted, on his 'Lucky Nights', as described by him, accompanied by the latest 'woman of fashion', at the *Rue Zeus* 'gambling hell' which attracts the 'over-rich *de Paris*' . . . Before disappearing — as described. Also, he believes it is not immoral to cheat at cards — and is said to have expressed the view the most 'poetic art' was the 'violent death of a beautiful woman'.'

Dupin took a drink of wine, while Lessiter stared at him, his brain crowded with shock and speculation.

'Would you say, Faith was a 'woman of fashion'?'

Dupin, who shrugged, 'Perhaps, because she is *not* . . . is the reason for her attraction . . . to him — ' He broke off, and looked away as if 'uneasy' to add anything more.

Lessiter, wrapped up in his own thoughts, failed to note the other's shadowed expression, 'I do find it impossible to believe — I never would have dreamed she was mixed up in all this . . . I mean, how did she meet him in the first place?'

Dupin, 'How did *you* meet her, in the first place — ?'

'Well, yes, I know — but one does meet people . . . at parties . . . the theater, etcetera . . . But Atherton — or, the *Duc de 'Whatever-His-Name-Is'* — spends much of his time in Paris — I didn't think his style of living would appeal to her.'

Aware the other must be reading what was churning round in his brain, he made an attempt at a shrug of the shoulders, as if to say, if that was the way it'd been — well . . . He broke off his thoughts and asked:

'And it's to do with him — Atherton, you're here — and, *Monsieur Gregoire?* Or, mustn't I ask — is it none of my blessed business?'

'*Monsieur* Gregoire, of the Paris *Surete*, is returned from Cairo. He preceded me to London.' At Lessiter's look of enquiry, Dupin continued: 'You may not have known it, but *Mademoiselle* Carteret has a cousin Derek Carteret, who in his capacity as *un Cairo Officer en civil* — a police officer — had obtained certain information, which he had passed to the Paris *Surete* . . . concerning strange 'creatures' living in an eastern region that had been believed uninhabited. But then . . . *he was found murdered!*'

Dupin paused to take a sip of wine — Lessiter hanging onto every word, face frozen with horror —

'I do believe you should, for your own

peace of mind, attempt to understand, even more to — to come to terms, as you English say, with the existence of such creatures as you have *ce soir* described — half-human — half-beetle ... And were able to persuade yourself it is the 'gift' they possess — Some may practice it, as you know, on the music-halls — at *Le Moulin Rouge* — or, your *Empire Music-Hall* — to cause audiences to believe in the impossible — and, if it is evil-intentioned, try by the Grace of God, to keep such evil at bay ... '

'You are actually saying this 'music-hall' performance put on *ce soir* for my benefit, was — was just trickery?'

Dupin shrugged, 'We are speaking about those from the East — men and women — who can live under the earth for many days and nights, to emerge unscathed — alive ... or, hold a blazing fire in the hand and not burn ... Be bitten by asps, vipers or poisonous spiders and not die — who can create shadows of individuals — *from other worlds — worlds unborn* ... '

'Like that chap this evening!'

Dupin nodded, 'Creatures from lost worlds, ancient wildernesses, deserts — from worlds outside our knowledge — where exists 'human' monsters from forgotten forests, from 'neath Ancient Seas . . . What do we know of their evil capabilities — ?'

'You — you — believe — such Things — actually existed? Or — *or exist today?*'

Dupin shrugged, 'I must tell you . . . *Monsieur Gregoire* of the Paris *Sureté* is returned from Cairo — with information . . . ' A pause, then: 'that there are those beyond that city — further East, who live in a nightmare out of Time — as they lived long ago . . . Like the most Evil Creatures of any tale of horror from the Ancient East — who are beyond the reach of Human Understanding — of Compassion . . . such *are* the *Beetles of Isis* . . . '

Pausing, as if to gain strength of resolve, so as he could continue,

'Let us go back in Time . . . Several tens of thousands of years — to a certain Saharan oasis — which is where . . . '
Leaning forward, as if to add weight, to

concentrate the listener's mind upon what he was saying, 'there was thrown up, from — from some secret Underworld, this — this *Unnamed Couple*, humans — some might say — except they had — these living creatures ... *Giant Beetles' heads* ... '

What was going through Lessiter's mind was:

So, *Inspector Gregoire — from the Paris Sureté* — is also involved with Dupin in this case? A thick-set individual, he recalled, always half-disguised in a heavy overcoat and hat over his eyes — a real plodding police-man — after the style, you might say, of the 'copper' who had spoken to him earlier on, on Chelsea Embankment ...

'One should mention,' the other was continuing, 'that the *Unnamed Couple* were male and female 'humans' ...Who —' A pause — 'duly begat further male and female humans ... ' Now, Dupin was staring at Lessiter, as if they were both together caught up in some horrific accident — '*avec* Giant Beetles' heads ...Thus there came about an *Underworld of thieves*

218

and assassins, *labeling* — *describing them-selves as* . . . the *Beetles of Isis* . . . who can twist themselves — you will note I use the present tense — into *shadows* . . . Or *creatures*, long since dead — Who may breathe as *humans*! *Mais* — what else can one believe . . . When it has been docu-mented . . . '

Lessiter watched as Dupin crossed to a well-stocked bookcase, the glass-door creaking as he opened it to take out a thick, age-battered volume, opening it at a well-worn page . . .

'Ah, *Latruelle* — ' from Lessiter, recognizing the volume's author . . . 'To whom you introduced me in Paris — '

Dupin nodded, 'One of several teachers of the Occult, whom I may quote with conviction,' pressing his right forefinger on the page, 'This is his description . . . ' Reading,

'*Scarabee* — Latin *Scarabaeus*: a Beetle, gold wings with a livid black spot, either side of its body . . . ''

'*A Beetle of Isis* — !' Lessiter said.

Dupin nodded, and read on, ''Once venerated at the ancient *Temple of Isis* by a — so-called — religious sect, who claimed they could transform themselves into beetles — very special beetles'.' A pause, and a long glance at Lessiter, then nodding at the age-browned page, continued, 'No metamorphosis — as in the case of pupa into the winged insect — but, directly . . . into animal — or human form . . . '

'Who practiced evil, murderous rites — ' from Lessiter, staring at Dupin, who, tapping the page, said: ' — it is believed, continue to breed . . . Traduit des mille anns . . . and would welcome fresh — blood . . . '

He put the book down, to reach for another age-battered volume off the shelf, Lessiter again noting its title,

'Ah . . . Les Maitres de L'Occultism — another ancient guide to Knowledge of the Distant Past . . . '

'And reference — ' Dupin, riffling through the age-crinkled pages, 'to Elicaster's illustrations, end of the book . . . Here we are — ' Stabbing the page with a forefinger — 'A hermaphrodite . . . A full-breasted creature — part female, part Beetle . . . '

He broke off and Lessiter stared at a Beetle's horrifically glinting head, large black spots either side, evilly slanting eyes above a graceful white neck, white curvaceous shoulders, and alluring breasts . . .

Dupin regarded him, eyes narrowed — *Lessiter's entire being* — *his very existence was suddenly shattered with sickening force, as he realized Faith's horrific fate* — *if she were not rescued from Atherton's obscenely gruesome grasp, illustrated so graphically by the female creature staring at him from Les Maitres de L'Occultism, in time . . .*

The front doorbell rang loud and strong. 'That will be Gregoire.' Dupin was heading for the hall. 'I asked him to report to us here . . . '

7

The large house, tall, dark trees either side of it, the wind whistling through them as the cab stopped outside the wide, black front door — two black panels shining like glass.

She'd been aware she was wearing a raincoat . . . and he had put the traveling-case between her and himself, which she had thought wasn't very . . . loving. She'd wanted him close to her — *loving her*. They were going on a journey together, weren't they? A long journey. To the East. They would travel on the *Orient Express*, from Paris to Cairo, where Derek had been killed.

Now, the clip-clop of the cab-horse receding, they were going up the path to the wide black door, and the wind whistled round her, so she shivered, hunching her shoulders, and pulling her coat round her and he was slightly behind her — he didn't help her with her coat. It was as if he wanted to be sure she wouldn't turn back.

The sound of the cab-horse's hooves had completely vanished as he opened the door for her, still keeping behind her — then followed her in.

She went through the dark hall — now, he was beside her, tall and dominating, heavy chin close to a thick, powerful neck . . . a *Prince of Power* — She was in a large room, which was illuminated by a glow, but there seemed to be no lamps: the ceiling was domed and the light shone down from it.

There was a large cigarette-box on an ornamental table, pushed against a huge divan — woven in gorgeous colors — and beetles — the same beetle, over and over . . . It was really a bedspread, covered with beetles. The same beetles, over and over.

The cigarette-box lid was gilt-decorated, with a huge beetle, gold-colored, a black blob on each of its two wings. She thought it gave the box an evil appearance . . . She saw Charles take a cigarette from it, light it and blew out a spiral of smoke . . .

It reminded her of when she was with him in Paris — One night he had taken her to an Egyptian Ballet at *L'Alhambra* — tales of Arabian nights with desert sands under the desert moon, were all the rage in Paris, and the show had all-Egyptian musicians, singers and dancers, song and dance — the big scene, the *Old Harem Secrets* — the stage filled with Egyptian dancing-girls . . . the theater filled with exotic 'Eastern perfume' and the smoke of Turkish, and Egyptian cigarettes . . . and people round her were saying some were smoking opium . . .

All very exotic and exciting — *strangely exciting* . . .

Then, she was suddenly unable to remember any more, and Charles had appeared once more, made to crush his cigarette under his heel, and stretched his arms, as if exerting himself to move forward, but remained rooted to the spot where he stood.

'I can't move,' he gasped. 'It won't let me.'

'What — what won't let you?' she

asked, low-voiced,

'*The Beetle* . . . Can you see it, now?'

Now, she heard, quite close to her — a buzzing sound.

She stared at him, then at where he was staring. Only, there was nothing to be seen . . . Now, he made another futile effort to move. He had become a feeble, frightened child.

He was seized with a kind of convulsion.

The spasm went as suddenly as it came, he stood in an attitude of expectancy, chin raised, head thrown back, eyes staring upwards, with a dreadful fixed glare, every faculty strained in the act of listening, not a muscle in his body moved, as rigid as a figure carved in stone.

Presently, the rigidity gave place to agitation.

'I hear,' he exclaimed, 'We are coming — !'

Now, a strange luminous glow filled the room. Everything became shadowed. Atherton stepped back from her, his still-burning cigarette a bright blob of light in the shadows.

Then, a sudden darkness, a total blackness, as if there had never been any light before.

And this sudden 'buzzing sound' over her head. The darkness and the total silence making the buzzing seem louder. Then, something — *Some Thing* — whatever it was — was approaching her, nearer and nearer and nearer.

Louder and louder.

It was overhead.

It dropped to the floor.

It was a beetle, huge and glittering. It stayed perfectly still, as she stared at it, her heart racing with fear . . . Premonition.

It remained still, motionless.

Then, she made it out in the darkness — this huge beetle, this strange glow about it.

She started to turn to speak to Atherton: What was all this about? Why weren't they making plans together to leave? To leave — for . . . For — for . . . ? For Cairo — where Derek, her cousin, was lying . . . dead. Why was he dead?

How had he died? Then, suddenly, there Charles was at the ornamental table, with the cigarette-box, the gold-colored beetle on its lid, the black blob on each wing . . . and he took out a cigarette — and now, there came a buzzing sound behind her. She swung round. Nothing. Only the darkness.

The buzzing sound was in front of her. She swung round again — now, two bright blobs of light were coming towards her.

The blobs of light vanished.

The buzzing sound was behind her again — she turned back again. The two blobs of light again — nearer — bigger.

Her heart began to race . . . She heard herself cry out,

'No — ! No — !'

She didn't know why she cried out — but the 'Thing' vanished — and now it was behind her once more.

It now looked as tall as herself. As tall as Charles — who was no longer there.

She wanted to turn away from this 'Thing', to call out to Charles — there was no one else she could call to . . . But she couldn't move. Couldn't speak.

The eyes came on, moving from side to side as if their owner walked unevenly.

Now, she realized the creature was beginning to climb her body.

It pressed against her; she felt the pressure of each leg, as they embraced her stickily — the creature glued and unglued each leg, each time it moved.

She perceived its outlines; it was slightly phosphorescent; it gleamed in the darkness. It grew heavier, so heavy, she wondered how, with so slight a pressure, it managed to retain its grip. It must do so by the aid of some sort of adhesive on its feet.

She became more and more conscious of an uncomfortable wobbling motion, as if each time it breathed, its body heaved.

Its forelegs touched her neck; they stuck to it and as it hung on with them, it drew its other legs up after it. It crawled up to her neck, with hideous slowness . . . It seemed a quarter-of-an-inch at a time.

It reached her chin, it touched her lips. She stood still — It enveloped her face with its huge, slimy, nauseatingly sweet-smelling body, and — and embraced her with its legs . . . It *was an embrace* as if the creature was — was physically attracted to her — wanted to — to — As she realized what it meant to do . . . she shook herself and the creature squashed upon the floor.

Then, it wasn't there — perhaps she'd half-fainted?

Instead . . .

Charles was standing before her again . . .

Only, was it Charles? Feet apart, broad shoulders set back, strong necked, heavy-jawed, handsome head shadowed, eyes glinting — suggestively heavy thighs, slim-waisted, now he leant forward, mouthing — she didn't recognize him,

'The Beetle . . . The Beetles of Isis!'

And she was filled with the conscious-ness of Evil . . . 'In God's name — *what* are you — ?'

He pulled out a handkerchief from his breast pocket, to dab his mouth. The 'Beetle' ring on his left little finger — the scarab with the jet-black spot either side — glittered as if it were alive.

'I must get you away — !' he muttered at her.

'To — to — to Cairo?' she asked. 'Cairo, you said we were going — !'

Suddenly, he yelled at her, 'Before you betray me — as your cousin betrayed me!'

''Betrayed you' — Derek?' She stared at him, terror-stricken . . .

'He was a spy! A police spy!'

Suddenly, she thought he was going to kill her — his eyes gleamed reddishly in the darkness —

His left hand caught her — *it looked like a claw*! His fingers had suddenly become 'talons' — they tore at her shoulder — tearing her dress — she felt a huge bruise spreading on her skin —

A knife — a curving blade — suddenly flashed in his right hand . . . *He was going to kill her where she stood* — !

He reached out with his other hand, holding her in such a way, her hands behind her back, while he hacked off her hair at the roots.

She shrieked in agony as the knife cut her scalp, her golden hair running with blood.

'So, you'll look like a younger cousin! You mustn't be recognized — ! That's who you are — a younger cousin — !'

The blood was running into her eyes.

He hacked her hair off again and again.

Yelling at her incoherently.

She heard herself screaming in agony. The blood ran into her mouth. She blacked out and fell.

He caught her before she hit the floor.

He stopped slashing at her hair.

He wiped the blood off her face — a handful of it.

8

Some half-an-hour later . . .

At the large dark house, under the tall black trees . . . Lessiter and Dupin were racing up in Gregoire's hansom which came to a hurried halt, the steam rising from the cab-horse, ghostly white — Gregoire had called urgently, reporting sharp and clear:

Mademoiselle Carteret could be found at 'Monsieur A's' Sloane Square house — unless, in his thick Parisian accent . . . 'Monsieur A' had left, avec Mademoiselle C. for the Continent and further East . . .

Now, 'Un moment,' to the cabbie, and Gregoire, hat over his eyes, and in his heavy overcoat, followed by Lessiter and Dupin, raced to the black front-door, quickly picking from his bunch of skeleton-keys, the one that clicked into place, a torch from his coat-pocket, then a pistol, led the way into the dark hall.

'Anyone at home . . . ?' from Lessiter. No reply . . .

Followed by Lessiter and Dupin, Gregoire led the way into the large room facing them, its door open — and his torch-light quickly swinging round, found the wall gas-lamps — matches flamed, the wall gas-lamps flamed, and the room came to life . . . The large gilt cigarette-box with its huge beetle on its lid on the ornamental table pushed against the wide divan, its cover in brilliant colors, beetles spread all over it . . . Then, the other side of the divan, the light, as if drawn with special urgency to the scene of horror, picked out chunks of blood-stained hair.

'*Mon Dieu — Mon Dieu*!' as Dupin went quickly to the mess, Lessiter overtaking him, crying out,

'It's hers — it's hers!' Turning to Dupin and Gregoire, 'She's been murdered — Atherton's murdered her — !'

'*Non — non —* !' from Dupin, 'She's *alive* — ! He wouldn't have taken a corpse — *Tres difficile* . . . to — to drag around with him — '

Lessiter stared at him uncomprehend-ingly.

'*Comprenez* — ? *He'll dress her up like a boy* — '

'So no one will recognize her,' from Gregoire.

Lessiter, 'Oh, yes . . . of course — So . . . where have they gone?'

'Wherever it is — ' Dupin, quickly crossing to where a crumpled time-table had fallen to the floor — '*it's by train* — ' grabbing the *British Railway Time-Table*, and, reading out,

'From *Charing Cross* — they go from *Charing Cross* — look — !' Holding out the time-table for Dupin to read — '*His blood-stained finger points to it* — '

Dupin, followed by Lessiter, whose face had drained to a ghastly ashen color, read where a blood-stained finger print marked the time-table:

'*Charing Cross — Harwich* — '

'Then: '10 . . . 55 p.m. — ' Lessiter read aloud — then, 'It would catch the boat for *The Hook* — and they'd be *en route* for *Cologne* . . . and on to *Istanbul* — for the East.'

Gregoire was nodding his head in agreement — But Dupin came in quickly,

'*Un moment!*'

His tone, a dagger-thrust. The other stared at him. He went on, 'It is an old trick — meant to deceive, so we will choose the wrong way — !'

Lessiter, face screwed up with anxiety — and Gregoire, 'What — What's wrong?'

Lessiter stared at him — was this a gamble?

'Take no notice of that attempt to distract us from the truth — ' Dupin's face taut with the certainty of intuition, 'She would not have been able to make a *finger-print of blood* — she'd be too weak . . . ' to Lessiter: 'You, as a doctor, would know that — ' and Lessiter nodded agreement. 'Something tells me it must be Victoria — I arrived there only this afternoon . . . there is a coincidence. There is a — a trick . . . in the scheme of things, a gift of intuition, when one knows . . . '

In his mind, Dupin was repeating the scene of his arrival. The cries of porters

— the noise of engines, the bustle of passengers. Intuitively, he knew, that vivid recollection had prompted his realization of the trick Atherton had attempted to dupe his pursuers. Turning quickly to Gregoiré,

'*N'est pas Charing Cross.* Telephone *Victoria — they will have the information . . .* ' and to Gregoire who was grunting agreement: 'A trick — marking a time-table, to show a false destination —!'

Gregoire was crossing quickly to a telephone, glinting in the gas-light on a side-table — grabbing it,

'I wish to speak to Victoria Railway-Station, *s'il vous plait* — quickly — quickly . . . '

Victoria Station lay in darkness — an occasional light making it even more Stygian — which, together with the lateness of the hour, suggested the station might be shut up for the night — but for the whistle of a departing train, and the echoing mutter of passengers' voices . . . While Dupin's reaction, as the hansom deposited him and Lessiter and clattered off, was that of disbelief . . . *Mon Dieu, hadn't he arrived from*

236

Paris this very afternoon — a coinci-dence . . .

He and Lessiter followed Gregoire — who was officially 'in charge of the investigation' — to the booking-office, their footsteps ringing out clearly, a door opening at their approach and the light within was thrown on their faces, as a voice called out,

'Who's that — ?'

Gregoire loudly introduced Lessiter and Dupin, and the voice responded,

'Step this way . . . '

The three visitors were inside the gas-lit office, and the tall, sturdy Railway-Inspector — 'I'm Jack Stone — what can I do to help you, gentlemen?' greeted them — it was he, Gregoire had spoken to on the phone, from the Sloane Garden's dark house of evil — and he went on,

'Reference the — er — 'Odd Couple', you're making inquiries about — ?' with a glance at Gregoire, who responded with a nod — 'A man — tallish, open-necked shirt? Accompanying a — er — young boy — '

A shout from Lessiter, 'That's her — !'

'Purchased two tickets — *First Class*,' Stone continued, 'destination Dover, and took the — ' breaking off to check a note on the desk before him — 'the 10.15 p.m.,' with a glance at his watch from his breast-pocket, 'Twenty minutes ago, that is — ' returning watch to pocket, and adding,

'Dover first stop . . . Next stop after that — the English Channel.'

There was a pause — a pause charged with tension, and his listeners couldn't help sensing it — it charged the very office-walls with such force.

'You say,' Lessiter put in, his voice rasping, 'the — *their* — train — with them in it — left twenty minutes ago?'

'*Thirty minutes, now . . .* '

'Where will it be — now?'

'Approaching Dartford — ' Another glance at the notes on his desk, 'Due there, 12.05.' Staring at Gregoire and Dupin, then giving a nod, 'I could alert Dartford police, who *could* have the train stopped . . . So they could hold the two passengers you're interested in — for questioning . . . ' He paused, then went

on, 'I say, '*could*' . . . but they might not
— without further — er — persuasion
from — er — higher authority — say,
Scotland Yard . . . ' He pursed his lips.
'They're not 'wanted' yet, you see
. . . Alternatively, let's check *Cross Channel* sailings . . . '

He pulled a dog-eared *Channel Sailings Time-Table* towards him, flipping
the pages quickly, paused and read, then,
from the side of his mouth,

'If your — er — couple arrive Dover in
time — they'll have two minutes to spare
— to nip aboard the *Dover Princess*,
departing for Calais.'

Stone heard a muttered exclamation,
and turned his head to observe Lessiter's
face stiffen and redden and his left hand
clench, so his knuckles whitened and
looked as if they must burst through the
skin. 'He must not get her across the
Channel — we will never catch them
— never — they will be lost.' Stone got to
his feet. 'Tell you what — will telegraph
Dover in time to alert local *gendarmerie*,'
with a grin and a wink at Gregoire, who
together with Dupin and Lessiter had also

stood up, 'to hold your couple on suspicion of whatever I can think up — that'll stop 'em from o'er the briny for foreign parts — '

He broke off, his expression turning grim, 'I mayn't get away with it — but it won't be for want of trying — !' Interrupting the other's expression of gratitude, plus Gregoire's grunt of approval, and continuing,

'Plus — will have engine-steam up — give us ten minutes — no, *seven* minutes — Dover's a fifty-mile run — with my driver's guts, plus a slice of luck, we should have you there on the heels of your couple . . . ' He'd picked up his 'phone — 'So you can nab 'em before they get aboard the '*Saucy Princess*' — and good luck!'

Now, his tone sharpened as he issued urgent and precise instructions into the 'phone.

9

What seemed less than a couple of minutes later, Stone was leading Dupin, Gregoire and Lessiter through the darkness, black sky overhead, chill wind off the Thames from Victoria Street, blowing into their faces, onto a low platform, to eye the black and glinting engine — behind it, a single coach — steam whistling up from its gross, gleaming body — coals in the cabin fire, reddening . . .

'Not quite *L'Orient Express*',' murmured Dupin.

'Well, you're not going to Constantinople — !' from Stone, calling up to the driver, a short, wiry man — gray hair, and grizzled moustache, leaning back from his engine, rubbing his hands with the usual oily rag,

'Told you — haven't I — ? Not to spare the coal — '

'Ought to do it,' the driver nodded.

'The gradients are against us — but 'tis a fog-clear night and no wind. Only thing that'll stop us will be if there's any shunting on the track, but you're the Guv'nor — '

Stone, emphatically, 'I'll clear the way for you — '

'Any stops *en route* to Dover, where they might get out?' Lessiter put in.

'Chatham and Faversham — '

'They won't,' said Gregoire — 'he's heading East, as M'sieur Dupin says.'

Dupin nodded.

'And Faith with him,' from Lessiter.

'So, full speed to Dover!' said Gregoire.

'If it should stop at Chatham, Police there will co-operate with you,' Stone assured them.

The engine gave a whistle.

'Come, come — Let us go ... ' Gregoire urged, and led the way into the middle compartment of the coach, Stone slamming the door, and calling after them, as the train pulled out,

'Bon chance — !'

'Indeed,' Gregoire yelled back, 'we shall need it — !'

'Only this coach? It's going to be a bumpy ride — ' from Lessiter. 'Well — so long as we arrive in time . . . ' Turning to Dupin, whom, he thought, was beginning to look a bit pale about the gills,

'Dupin — you all right?'

'I — er — I'm not used to traveling — in — in this style — ' his mind again returning to his earlier, uneventful arrival at Victoria from Dover.

'Sit with your back to the engine — ' Gregoire advised.

'Ah, yes — '

'Never worries me,' Gregoire added.

The train sped along.

'It's still hellish dark,' Lessiter observed.

'We will see the dawn soon — ' Dupin offered . . . 'In every sense — one hopes,' he murmured.

The coach shook from side to side as the speed increased.

'Piling on the coal,' Gregoire muttered.

'Hope we don't jump the rails . . . ' from Lessiter. 'Feeling better, Dupin?' Louder, 'Feeling better?'

Dupin responded with a slight nod.

Racing along by a single train-coach

attached to an engine flying at topmost speed is very different from traveling by ordinary express . . . Quite apart from the difficulty keeping their seats, when every moment the three of them were jerked backwards and forwards, up and down, this way and that, was the deafening noise, as deafening as if they were being pursued by a legion of raging demons.

Philosophically, Dupin decided the very severity of the discomfort he was suffering served to divert his mind from the dread thought that absorbed him to the exclusion of all else . . .

Onwards — onwards, the train, roaring, rumbling.

Lessiter, who had been endeavoring every now and then to peer through the window, strained his lungs again in the effort to make himself heard,

'Where the devil are we?'

'It's nearly one o'clock,' from Gregoire — who'd been wishing — *Mon Dieu* — they'd gone to the Hook — it might have been less bumpy! Looking at his watch, 'I suppose we're somewhere in the neighborhood of — ' The rest of his sentence was drowned by a shriek from the engine.

A further several moments roared past, then came a shrill whistle . . . then the grinding application of brakes.

Simultaneously, all three were on their feet.

Lessiter let down a window and quickly shouted back,

'Looks as if the line's blocked — or else we've stopped — Chatham — or, it could be Faversham — '

Gregoire, '*Mais c'est impossible* — ! We can't be there yet — !'

The train-brakes screeched horrifically. Dupin relaxed a little, 'Aren't we slowing down?'

'We're stopping,' was all he got from Dupin, voice full of relief, which he didn't take the trouble to disguise.

'See if I can make out what's going on,' Lessiter said, pulling the compartment window down. 'Something's on the line!' he shouted back. 'I can't see . . . '

The train was slowing to a halt.

They shouted together, 'Are we at a station?'

'No,' Lessiter said, 'not at any station . . . '

'An accident on the line?' Dupin queried.

'We'll never reach Dover — ' from Gregoire, voice charged with furious exasperation. 'Something's up! We've stopped. Someone waving a lamp — !'

'Let me look . . . ' Gregoire grunted. 'The line is blocked — '

Lessiter shouted, 'What's wrong, driver?'

'Tree fallen across the track,' a voice came back — 'Train smashed into it.'

'*The one ahead of us* — ?' from Dupin.

'It's *their* train — ' Lessiter came in urgently.

'*Vitement! Vitement* — ! They'll get away.'

Lessiter turned to Dupin to give him a hand — they both jumped down . . . And from Lessiter, 'It certainly can't be Dover . . . '

10

It wasn't Dover — so much seemed clear.

The collision had put out all the carriage lamps — there were the glimmer of matches . . . these were all the lights that shone upon the scene.

Though at first, none of the three could make out anything — Lessiter was feeling dazed, there was a singing in his ears, the darkness seemed impenetrable — as their eyes drew accustomed to the darkness, they became aware someone was making what haste they could along the six-foot way, swinging a warning red lamp.

'What's the matter?' the engine-driver called out from his cabin, 'Who's that?'

It was the guard from the other train,

'My God . . . You were coming right on top of us — !'

'What — what's wrong?' the engine-driver climbing down to the track, 'I thought you were on the 12.00 out — we're chasing you.'

But Dupin had quietly moved off, with sudden instinctive speed, face set purposefully — sure-footed now as a cat, body tense, tilted in a sudden alertness, seeking some answer to — to some conundrum.

He is alongside the other train, its great engine — like some frustrated beast, gasping gray steam up into the night — *and sees a massive black tree trunk, and branches, which had crashed down, effectively blocking the path* . . . And his eyes are drawn up to trees grouped atop the embankment — and a huge phosphorescent shape. Lessiter's 'Beetle' — the Priest of Isis — his gaze, even in the darkness, aflame with triumph, riveted on him — as he screeches down:

'I have saved her — saved her Life and very Soul — !'

And Dupin knows — hair rising from his scalp — heart racing — knows, *sans l'ombre d'un doute* — ! This Dark Priest, by some strange 'witchcraft', had caused that great black tree to crash down — effectively blocking Atherton's race with Faith Carteret across the Channel, *en route* to the Farthest East . . . and an Enormity of Evil . . . Then, suddenly this rush of air, *as if the sound of beating phosphorescent wings* — and the dark figure had gone.

Instantly, Dupin turns to hasten back, to find Lessiter and Gregoire helping free some passengers forcibly locked in their compartments by the collision's impact.

The passengers had mostly succeeded in freeing themselves, but some were still imprisoned, and there were appeals for help.

'Open the door . . . '

'In the name of God . . . Open the door . . . '

Lessiter calling out, 'Anyone hurt?'

Guard, coming in, 'Not many passengers — one carriage turned right over — Young boy killed — !' he added.

Dupin, 'A boy — ?'

'Poor little devil — ' The guard, shaking his head.

'Faith!' Lessiter forced out the name.

'Killed outright — ' the driver continued.

'Dupin — come on . . . ' Lessiter urged.

'Only the boy?' from Gregoire, 'but the man — ?'

'Let me get into the compartment,' said Lessiter. 'I'm a doctor . . . perhaps I can . . . ' His voice died away.

'Get this door open — it's jammed . . . ' from the driver.

'Pull — that's it!' Gregoire and the driver wrenched open the compartment-door and, followed by the others, scrambled in. By the light of Gregoire's torch, they made out — sprawled in a corner — the body of what appeared to be a young boy . . . ragged hair covered with blood.

'*Mademoiselle* Carteret — ' Dupin said.

Lessiter's head was close to her heart, 'It's all right . . . she's alive — it's all right — I'll carry her . . . She's very light . . . ' He was already holding her in his arms, tears of relief streaming down his face, and muttering, 'Thanks to you, Dupin . . . Thanks to you — '

'Our man's escaped, in the darkness — ' Dupin to the driver — in the confusion.'

'What's that — on the floor?' the driver wanted to know.

'Your lamp — ' Dupin urgently.

'Here you are — '

From Gregoire, 'I'll find him — if I have to go to the ends of the earth. What is it — ?'

'It looks like a lot of blood . . . but it isn't — ' observed Dupin.

'Nasty-looking mess . . . ' Gregoire agreed.

Dupin, 'It's oily, viscous . . . Ugh!'

'Like some huge, squashed beetle — ' from Gregoire.

There was a buzzing of a beetle.

'What's that — ?' Dupin's voice suddenly a gasp of horror.

'Beetle — horrible thing — kill it!'

'It's gone . . . ' said Dupin.

More buzzing, very loud — then receding . . .

'*The Beetle* . . . ' Dupin, half to himself. 'It will return — No, it must not — '

'What's that?' Gregoire asked. 'What, Monsieur Dupin — ?'

'No, it must not . . . *Non — non* . . . ' again from Dupin.

What had transpired in that railway compartment during that fated moment of collision . . . may never be known . . .

It seemed to Dupin on the evidence in the compartment itself, Faith Carteret, having endured what can only be described as a cataleptic trance — and so devastated by what she could only believe to have been some dreadful nightmare — was incapable of describing the phantasmagoric terror she'd endured during those fateful hours. She was under medical care for several months before, finally, recovering from her ordeal. How fully, one was never made aware.

Dr. Lessiter? Desperately in love with Faith Carteret, he was persuaded by Dupin that to press his suit with her would actually be harmful. It was clear to Dupin, as a student of psychology and the human mind, that to aid her recovery, the girl's subconscious mind had suppressed the memories of her recent horrific experiences with Atherton and the death of her cousin, *and these buried memories included Lessiter's proposal*! Were Lessiter to propose to her again, he would undoubtedly trigger her buried memories of Atherton's atrocities. That could set back the girl's recovery.

Clearly *Mademoiselle* Carteret needed to be free from all mental stress and close medical care for some considerable time to come. The noble Lessiter had therefore agreed to leave it to healing time to tell whether or not he should offer the girl his love again.

And Atherton — *alias* the *Duc de Xancr?* He who had abducted Faith Carteret for unimaginably evil purposes . . . ? Nothing further remains to be reported concerning him; to this hour, nothing concerning him — or his involvement with the *Beetles of Isis* — is known.

And the 'Priest'? Lessiter's dark — menacing — visitor Out of the Night . . . Priest of the *Beetles of Isis* . . . who warned Lessiter against Atherton's Evil Powers — which would rob him of the woman he loved — and, like Atherton, changed himself into this obscenely horrible Beetle and, like Atherton . . . Still lives . . . ?

As for Derek Carteret — 'Cause of Death' remains unsolved; Faith Carteret never referred to it, and perhaps, never will?

And so, Dear Reader, with what

knowledge I possess of the East's Ancient Worlds, I, Auguste Dupin, am positive that the events which I have so far described and have reconstructed were — I have no doubt — the manifestations of some Evil Force from a truly forgotten, unimaginably venomous past — which still survives.

And which one day may return.

THE END

We do hope that you have enjoyed reading this large print book.

Did you know that all of our titles are available for purchase?

We publish a wide range of high quality large print books including:
Romances, Mysteries, Classics
General Fiction
Non Fiction and Westerns

Special interest titles available in large print are:
The Little Oxford Dictionary
Music Book, Song Book
Hymn Book, Service Book

Also available from us courtesy of Oxford University Press:
Young Readers' Dictionary
(large print edition)
Young Readers' Thesaurus
(large print edition)

For further information or a free brochure, please contact us at:
Ulverscroft Large Print Books Ltd.,
The Green, Bradgate Road, Anstey,
Leicester, LE7 7FU, England.
Tel: (00 44) **0116 236 4325**
Fax: (00 44) **0116 234 0205**

Other titles in the
Linford Mystery Library:

TO DREAM AGAIN

E. C. Tubb

Ralph Mancini, an officer in the United Nations Law Enforcement Agency, is dedicated to the world-wide War on Drugs. A new drug is developed, giving a uniquely effective 'trip', whereby people become God-like beings and they experience 'heaven'. The next trip is their only priority — whatever the cost. Ralph and Inspector Frere follow a tangled trail of murder, seeking the source of the peril — but will they be too late to stop it spreading across the world?